THE BILLIONAIRE'S CHRISTMAS MIRACLE

A CHRISTIAN BILLIONAIRE ROMANCE

LORANA HOOPES

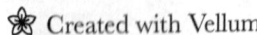 Created with Vellum

NOTE FROM THE AUTHOR

Thank you so much for picking up this book. I hope you enjoy the story and the characters as they are dear to my heart. If you do, please leave a review at your retailer. It really does make a difference because it lets people make an informed decision about books.

Sign up for Lorana Hoopes's newsletter and get her book, The Billionaire's Impromptu Bet, as a welcome gift. Get Started Now!

Lorana's Other Billionaire Books:

The Billionaire's Secret

Brush With a Billionaire

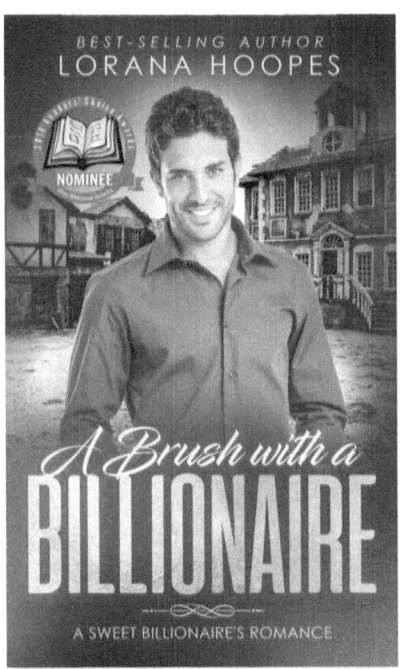

The Billionaire's Cowboy Groom

The Cowboy Billionaire coming soon

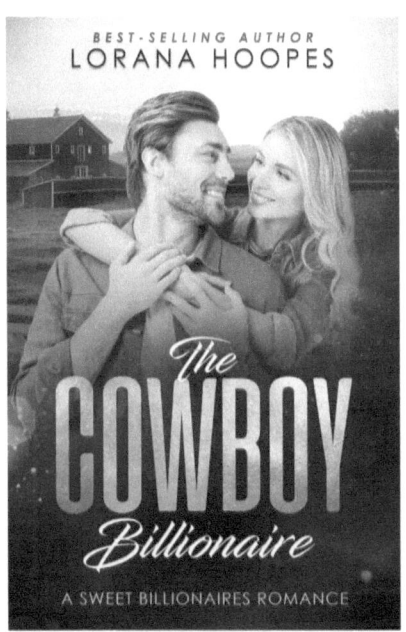

The COWBOY Billionaire

A SWEET BILLIONAIRES ROMANCE

CHAPTER 1

*G*wen's jaw dropped as she regarded her friend. Surely, she had misheard Carrie's request. There was no way she could be serious. "You want me to do what?" Didn't Carrie understand what she was asking was one of Gwen's worst nightmares?

"Pretend to be me." Carrie flicked her fiery red hair off her shoulder and picked up the eyeshadow brush. She swiped it across her lid, nonchalantly, as if she had just been asking Gwen to hand her a shirt and not walk into a room full of strangers. Strangers!

"Just for the night. I'm so tired of these parties, and I promised Lorenzo I'd go riding with him." Lorenzo was Carrie's latest fling - a tall, dark, Italian bad boy who wore leather and drove a Harley. At least Gwen was fairly certain his name was Lorenzo. Carrie Bliss changed men like most people changed socks, and she had a hard time keeping up.

While Gwen adored Carrie, she often wondered how

they were still friends. In college, it had made sense. Gwen was the studious library aide and Carrie was the sorority girl who needed help on her papers. But now? Carrie owned her own business and was steadily climbing the "Who's who in society" ladder while Gwen was an ordinary English teacher. A teacher who had nightmares every year about meeting the upcoming class of students, but they were just kids. Kids like she had been once who needed help, so she could swallow her fear of strangers and stand up in front of them, but she could not walk into a party with a bunch of wealthy adults. Carrie knew this.

"But we don't look alike," Gwen protested with a shake of her head. That wasn't exactly true. They had been mistaken for sisters more than once, but she needed an excuse. Any excuse.

Carrie set the make-up down and turned to Gwen. Her right eyebrow inched up her forehead in a stop-being-a-baby expression. "We look close enough. We both have red hair, we're about the same height-"

"You're two sizes smaller than me," Gwen finished. She wasn't overweight, but her size eight to ten frame was bigger than Carrie's perfect size six one.

Carrie flashed her manicured hand in a dismissive wave. French tips. They were so pretty. Gwen's own nails were all different lengths and not painted. She'd only had one manicure in her life. High school prom. Her foster mother had taken her to get a manicure even though she didn't have a date. "Everyone should feel pretty at least one day," she'd said. Carrie, on the other hand, had a weekly standing appointment with her nail lady, and while she'd offered to take Gwen along and pay for hers more than once, Gwen just couldn't do it. It seemed like a frivolous waste of money even if it wasn't her money.

"Just don't get too close to anyone, and no one will know. Besides, most of these people barely know me. They just know the name of Carrie Bliss Designs. The only one you'd have to watch out for is Grant." Her nose wrinkled the tiniest bit as she said his name.

Grant was Carrie's ex - a snobby stock broker who managed the portfolios of many of the wealthiest in the city. Gwen had never liked Grant nor understood why Carrie dated him, but then again, she didn't understand why Carrie dated half the men she did. "I don't know, Carrie, it's not really my thing."

"Which is exactly why you should go." Carrie turned back to the mirror and puckered her lips. "You never do anything fun. You go to work and then you come home and hang out there."

That part was true; Gwen's life was boring, but she liked it that way. At least most days. "I'm a homebody. I like staying home." Plus, it was safer there. No one would beat her or die on her if she stayed in her house. Yes, it was lonely on occasion, but still safer.

Carrie's eyes flicked up to catch Gwen's in the mirror. "But you'll never meet anyone stuck inside this house."

Which was the whole point. Gwen didn't want to meet someone. It hurt too much to love people.

"Besides, this is the perfect opportunity," Carrie

continued, "you'll be wearing a mask, so you can hide behind it."

Gwen's teeth bit into her bottom lip. Wearing the mask might make it better. It wouldn't curb her anxiety about being in a room full of strangers, but it would help that they couldn't really see her. And it would be something different. "What will I wear?" Gwen couldn't believe she was even considering this. "Is it formal? Because I have nothing formal."

"Relax, I'm sure I have something in my closet that will fit you. Come on, let's go look."

She followed Carrie to her immense closet. Though they had shared an apartment for a time in college, eventually Carrie's more expensive taste and wallet had led her to purchase a penthouse in the city. Gwen, however, rented a studio in a much poorer section of town.

"Let's see." Carrie walked along the dresses hanging down, her hand touching each garment as she passed. Gwen would never get used to the size of this closet. It was nearly the size of her whole apartment. Carrie stopped and pulled out an emerald green gown. "Try this one. I remember it being slightly big on me, so it's probably just your size."

Gwen's fingers touched the satiny gown. It was more expensive than anything she would ever own. Off the shoulder and floor length, the satin rippled like waves as it fell to the floor. "What if I ruin it?" Gwen wasn't exactly a klutz, but she could just picture herself spilling a fancy drink on the beautiful gown.

Carrie smiled. "You won't, and even if you do, it's not

like I'm hurting for it." She gestured to the myriad of dresses still hanging on the rods.

She was running out of excuses, and it was just one night. Perhaps it would even be fun, and she could reminisce on the evening later when the silence pressed in on her at her apartment. It wasn't like she would have another chance at something like this. "Okay, I'll see if it fits."

Carrie stepped out of the closet to give Gwen some privacy. She laid the gown across the padded bench and shook her head. Who had a bench in their closet? She didn't think she would ever get used to some of the things wealthy people seemed to waste their money on.

Her fingers trembled slightly as she removed her clothes and stepped into the dress. *This is wrong* paraded again and again in her head like a scratched record, but her hands still pulled the dress up. Her fingers still found the zipper and tugged. It was a little snug, but it fit. If she didn't eat too much.

Lifting the dress so as not to step on the hem, Gwen stepped out of the closet. Carrie clapped her hands and sighed. "Yes, you look perfect. Well, almost perfect. Hang on." She hurried back into the closet and the sound of drawers opening and closing carried out. "Ah, here we go." She re-emerged holding a feathered mask and held it out. "Now, you'll look perfect."

Gwen's fingers grasped the mask, a beautiful atrocity of purples, greens, and golds. She pulled the string and fastened it over her face before turning to the mirror. Whoa! Her lips parted at the vision in front of her, and a small gasp escaped.

She looked... beautiful, and Carrie was right - no one would know it wasn't Carrie from far away. With her face covered, she appeared even more like her friend.

"See? I told you. Now let's get you some shoes, a little jewelry, and pin your hair up."

Gwen glanced down at her wrist. "Can I keep the bracelet on at least?" It was the last thing her parents had given her - a diamond tennis bracelet. And it never came off, not even to shower.

Carrie's eyes softened. She had never met Gwen's parents - they had been dead for years before Carrie entered the picture, but Gwen had told her about them one late night over popcorn and The Breakfast Club. "I'd never ask you to take your bracelet off. I was just thinking some diamond earrings would be a great match with it."

Tears filled Gwen's eyes. *This* was why she and Carrie were still friends. Though worlds apart, she was so thoughtful sometimes.

With the earrings picked and the shoes found, Gwen checked the mirror one last time. She still couldn't believe she was doing this, but she might as well make the most of it. For one night, she could pretend to be Carrie, pretend to be wanted, pretend to be wealthy and not have a care in the world. It was just one night.

*D*rew Devonshire adjusted his mask. He looked a little like the Phantom with his white shirt, dark pants, and cape, but the look suited him. If only he were more excited about this event, but they were all the same. He'd been attending them for years, and the results never changed. By the end of the night, he would be dying of boredom, dazed from the alcohol he'd consumed to battle said boredom, and have at least a dozen numbers in his pocket from women after his money whom he had no interest in.

It was always the same people there - the affluent and elite of society. They would gather at some elaborate venue with tiny portions of intricate food that would cost whoever was hosting the event a fortune. In this case, that was Drew, or his family rather, as his mother was hosting this masquerade ball at one of their hotels.

Occasionally, a millionaire from another town would be in attendance or sometimes a relative of one of the families would be, but even those instances were rare. His mother invited old friends and only new people she thought would attend her next benefit. Since those were priced at a thousand dollars a plate that list was small. Plus, while the food was delectable, it never filled him up, and he invariably had to have his chef make him a second meal when he returned home.

If only he could get out of this, but his mother would be there. If he didn't attend, she would be livid. As heir to the billion-dollar hotel chain, it was his duty to attend events like this. Maybe he could leave early, but what would he do even if he could? Return home to his mansion and watch television alone again? He already did that nightly.

For a time, he had filled his nights with women. One after the other, he had wined them and dined them, but none had held his interest. Soon, the very thought of dating and pretending to like them had grown old. They were all alike - cookie cutters of their mothers and their mothers before them. Tailored clothing, designer shoes, and an appetite for spending money without abandonment appeared to be all that drove these women. Drew wanted something different. He had no idea what, but something different. No, that wasn't true. He wanted someone like Marjorie had been or who he thought Marjorie had been.

A knock sounded on his door. "Come in." It had to be Pierre, his butler. Though officially the help, Pierre felt more like family. He had been Drew's butler for over a decade now and his confidante almost as long.

"Are you ready, sir? Manuel has the limo waiting." Pierre was older than Drew, gray at the temples and with more lines on his face, but still handsome. He had never wanted to marry, and as Drew paid him well, he seemed content to remain Drew's main butler, but he had a few men beneath him, so he could take time off when he needed.

Drew sighed. It wasn't as if he had much choice. "I suppose I am." He shoved his wallet in his pocket. "Pierre, is there anything else going on tonight? If I finish early?"

Pierre's brows knitted together. "Early, sir? Don't these events run on the lengthy side?"

"Yes, they do, but I was thinking about retiring early." He hoped Pierre was catching his innuendo. "If something else were going on that sounded interesting, I mean."

Pierre nodded. "Ah, I see. I'm afraid I am not well informed on the night life around town, but Manuel usually has knowledge of such events. Although I must say, the Devonshire events are always the talk of the town, so I'm not sure what else you might be looking for."

That elicited a small smile from Drew. He clapped Pierre on the shoulder. "Me either, but thank you, my friend. I will ask Manuel."

"Very good, sir." Pierre nodded and stepped out of the way, so Drew could exit the room.

Though he lived alone, except for the help he employed, his mansion was palatial. Five bedrooms each with their own bathroom took up the second floor. A large grandiose stairway connected the two floors, and his loafers clicked against the white marble as he made his way down them.

The stairs ended in the grand foyer, a room as large as most people's living rooms with the sole purpose of connecting the front door to the living room. A single closet to hang coats in and a hat rack which held his hat and scarf were the only things in the room besides a mirror that hung on one wall.

After donning his hat and wrapping his scarf around his neck, Drew checked his reflection in this mirror. The image reflecting back was dapper if he did say so himself. He flung open the front door to find Manuel waiting on the porch.

"Are you ready, sir?" Manuel was much younger than

Pierre. Younger than Drew even, but he'd come highly recommended after Drew's last driver had run off with Marjorie. And so far, Drew had no complaints. Manuel always dressed immaculately, he drove the speed limit, and he kept the limo stocked with Drew's favorite snacks - beef jerky and Doritos.

Not the typical fare for a billionaire, but then Drew wasn't the typical billionaire. He didn't like the taste of Dom Perignon, and caviar held no appeal for him either. While the help and the limo were nice, sometimes he wished he could just go camping in the woods with some burger patties, hot dogs, and chips.

His mother hated that side of him. "We should never have allowed you to go off to a regular college," she reminded him often, but Drew was glad he'd gotten the chance to see how the other half lived. In fact, he'd wanted to do something other than inherit a billion-dollar hotel industry, but when his father died, he'd been forced to step into his shoes.

"As ready as I'll ever be, I suppose," Drew said as he followed Manuel to the long black car.

Manuel nodded as if he understood what Drew meant though Drew knew he did not understand. People thought they wanted to be wealthy, but they had no idea the taxing monotony it carried with it. He always had to be dressed when he went outside. One poorly chosen outfit and his face would end up splashed across the tabloids within hours. Dates needed to be well planned out, and he could never say what he was thinking. Having to always be diplomatic required constant attention and control. And Drew was tired of it.

Plus, there was the prying into his private life. After Marjorie had run away with the chauffeur, he had been the talk of every tabloid. It was only after a fellow heiress had gotten herself arrested for driving intoxicated that he had faded from the public scrutiny and pity.

"Manuel, if I wanted to leave the ball early, would you know of any place that might have something of interest going on tonight?"

Manuel pursed his lips. "Do you mean of the local nightlife variety?"

Drew slid into the leather seat and nodded. "That is precisely what I mean."

"I have heard nothing other than the talk of this masquerade ball."

Drew sighed. Of course, he hadn't. Drew's mother did her best to make sure her parties conflicted with nothing and garnered all the attention. "I was afraid of that, but do me a favor, will you, Manuel? Keep your ears open in case something comes up."

Manuel nodded. "I will do my best, sir." Then he shut the door and Drew was left alone in the dimly lit interior of the limo.

CHAPTER 2

G wen stepped out of the limo and looked up at the massive hotel rising against the moonlit sky. It was one of the largest in the city, and though she knew of it by name, she had never been inside. Why would she? One night's stay in this place probably cost a week's worth of her pay.

"Thank you," she said to Carrie's driver as he held the door open for her. The man blinked at her and nodded. Was he surprised? Did Carrie never thank him? Maybe she was just too used to the service or in too much of a hurry, but Gwen was neither. She was still unsure she wanted to go through with this, but a tremor of excitement flickered inside her.

The limo door closed behind her, and the sound caused her to jump. She was too skittish. Then a chill swept through the area, and Gwen pulled her shawl tighter across her shoulders. Winter was on its way, and as the limo had just pulled out, her only options were to enter the building or stand outside on the cold, dark sidewalk. The latter held no appeal.

Before she had time to change her mind, her feet carried her across the pavement. Orange and red leaves from nearby trees squished under her shoes, still wet from the most recent rain. She took a moment to rub her feet across the red carpet that rolled out of the hotel and under the large awning. Tracking wet leaves into the hotel would surely be frowned upon. A bellhop, dressed in maroon and gold, smiled and held the door open for her, and Gwen stepped inside.

She clamped her lips together to keep her jaw from dropping. The inside of the hotel dripped with opulence, but someone with Carrie's money probably wouldn't have thought twice about it. A vein of gold ran through the marble flooring and carried up the walls and across the ceiling. An enormous chandelier hung from the middle of the room sending rainbows of color cascading across the area, and one wall held a fountain apparatus that made it appear water flowed down the wall. Gwen had never seen such a beautiful room.

"Can I help you?" The deep, velvety voice came from behind her.

Gwen pulled her shoulders back hoping to appear confident as she turned to the masculine voice. A man wearing a white shirt, black pants, and a cape stared back at her. A large mask hid most of his facial features, but Gwen saw his icy blue eyes and his perfect lips beneath the mask.

Her stomach clenched, and she forced her voice to sound

even and not the jittery mess she felt inside. "Um, I'm here for the Masquerade Ball."

His lips turned up at the corners, hinting at the sexy smile that could follow. "Well, as fate would have it, so am I. May I show you the way?"

Gwen's heart raced in her chest. She wanted to go with him, this Adonis, but he was a strange man, and if foster care had taught her anything, it was that she couldn't trust everyone. "I…"

Now his lips pulled into that smile, and it was even more charming than Gwen had pictured. "I understand your hesitation." He leaned in and glanced around. "I'm Drew Devonshire." He paused as if waiting for that to mean something to her, but his name meant nothing. Was she supposed to know him? Was he famous? "This is my hotel."

The light went off in her head. The Devonshire Hotel, of course, but was he really a Devonshire or some con man just pretending so he could lure her off somewhere? Gwen shook her head. She needed to get her morbid ideas in check. Not everyone was out to get her. He appeared perfectly respectable, and this *was* a public hotel. However, stories of people killed in hotels littered the internet, and she'd read H. H. Holmes built one for that very reason. She took a deep breath and swallowed her inane fears. "I'd be honored to have you lead the way to the ball."

"Wonderful, follow me." He led the way across the marbled foyer to the hallway where four gold plated elevators waited, two on each side of the hallway. A circular button with an up arrow sat in between each door. The man pushed the button, and a moment later when the door of one opened, he stepped inside.

"Are you coming?" His voice held a teasing note, and though she couldn't see it, Gwen imagined his eyebrow was lifted. He probably wasn't used to indecisive rich women.

Gwen paused for just a moment, knowing she was blowing her cover, but unable to help it. Once she stepped into the small box, she would be at his mercy. Surely the ride would be short though, and a hotel this big had video cameras. "Um, yeah, sorry." She joined him inside and tried not to show her apprehension as the doors slid closed. Her hands clenched her shawl tighter to keep from shaking.

"Not a fan of elevators, huh?"

Gwen looked down. "Oh, no, it's not that. It's...." but she couldn't tell him her fear was of strangers. Men, in particular. Fearing strangers was a child's fear, not a grown woman's one and certainly not a fear of a famous designer. So, she said the first thing she could think of. "I don't like small spaces." It wasn't a complete lie. Gwen preferred open areas where the option to run existed.

"Hmm." He stared at her as if trying to gauge if she was telling the truth or not. "Well, that is understandable." A pause ensued as if he wanted to press the subject more, but finally he nodded and then leaned in towards her as if sharing a secret. "So, I understand this is a masquerade ball and sharing our identities is discouraged, but since I told you who I am, can I at least get your name?"

Gwen didn't want to state her actual name in case a guest list existed she wouldn't be on, but it felt wrong telling him Carrie's name as well. What if he tried to look her up later? Perhaps if she just gave a first name, it would be okay. "It's Carrie, but that's all I'm saying." She hoped she sounded coy, but she feared the lie was evident in her voice.

"Well, I'll take what I can get." He nodded and flashed another small smile as the doors opened. With a flourishing gesture, he held out his arm for her to go first, and Gwen stepped out of the elevator.

Her heart sank as she saw a large man with a clipboard standing outside the door. He was obviously checking names off a list, which would be fine as long as he didn't know the real Carrie Bliss. But a stack of cards sat on the table beside him. Invitations? Carrie had said nothing about bringing an invitation, and Gwen didn't have one. Had she gotten all dressed up only to be turned away at the door?

"Invitations?" the man asked as they approached.

"I, um, don't have one, but I should be on the list," Gwen mumbled.

"No invitation, no entry." The man crossed his arms sending the sleeves of his suit bulging with the motion. He might look fancy, but he was obviously a bouncer who wouldn't be afraid to throw a little muscle around if needed.

"Well, I have no invitation either, but I would hate to inform my mother you denied her son, Drew Devonshire, entrance into his own event." He lifted his mask, and the guard's demeanor instantly changed.

"I'm sorry, Mr. Devonshire, sir, I didn't recognize you. Of course, you don't need an invitation."

Drew nodded. "Thank you, and neither does my friend. I'll vouch for her."

Indecision crossed the guard's face. He looked from Drew to Gwen and back again. "All right, sir, if you're sure."

"I am." Drew held out his hand to Gwen. "Carrie? Shall we?"

Suddenly, Gwen grew nervous for a new reason. Clearly, the man before her was Drew Devonshire which meant he did own the hotel. He wasn't likely to harm her, but what if he realized she wasn't who she said she was? Would he throw her out? Call security? Call the police? She would just have to be careful what she said and did.

She placed her hand in his. A tingling sensation raced up her arm at his touch, and she looked down at their hands. How long had it been since a man had touched her? The answer was ages. Gwen didn't allow most men to touch her, at least not until she knew they were safe and not like the first foster father she'd had. And though she dated, she was cautious and picky in her choices. First dates rarely turned in to second ones.

When she looked back up, Drew was staring at her. "Ready?" he asked.

Gwen nodded, not trusting her voice. She was probably already sending out many signs she wasn't the wealthy elite she was pretending to be, but she knew if she opened her mouth and her voice quivered, he would glean that information for sure. Carrie never seemed unsure of herself though whether that was due to her money or just Carrie's personality Gwen wasn't sure.

Drew opened the door to the ballroom. Just like downstairs, the room was elegant and refined, and Gwen had to force herself not to stare as she took everything in.

*D*rew watched as Carrie's eyes widened when they entered the room. He was used to such elaborate decor, but her expression revealed that she wasn't. Though she fought to keep her face composed, he could tell the room awed her. And she'd been standing downstairs like a scared rabbit. He wondered if she would have stood in the lobby all night if he hadn't approached her. Plus, she'd had no invitation though she'd claimed to be on the list. Could she be a new millionaire, maybe? Or a relative of someone? Either way, she intrigued him. Perhaps this evening wouldn't be so bad after all.

"Would you care to dance?" he asked her as they stepped farther into the room. Couples already filled the dance floor while others lingered at the tables around the room.

Her eyes dropped to the floor. "I'm not much of a dancer," she said in a soft voice. What was this lack of self-confidence she exuded? It was not typical for people with money.

"Lucky for you, I am." He flashed a smile as he pulled her to the middle of the dance floor. "My mother made me take a year of ballroom dancing lessons. I might as well put them to good use." Drew wrapped an arm around her waist and cinched her closer. Not only did she fit nicely in the crook of his arm, but the sweet smell of vanilla drifted up from her. He wasn't sure if it came from her hair or her skin, but he enjoyed the scent.

She followed his steps but felt stiff in his arms. Had she had no dance training? Not that everyone of wealth did, but it was standard practice among the elite. Perhaps she had only recently become wealthy. One of the rising stars his mother had invited?

"Did you enjoy them?" she asked.

"What? Oh, the lessons?" She nodded. "Not really, but when you are a Devonshire, there are rules you have to follow."

"There are always rules," she said.

"That is true, but our rules are stricter than most. Surely, you must have similar experiences." He fixed his eyes on her as he waited for her answer.

"Oh, um, sure, you know always wear the right outfit and makeup, things like that, but we didn't have to dance." She glanced up at him before her eyes shifted to the side. Clearly, she was hiding something, but what? And, more importantly, why?

"What do you do?" he asked changing the subject and hoping to elicit a little information from her.

Carrie cleared her throat and her eyes flicked around the room. Everywhere but on him. "I um run my own business."

Interesting. Drew had become adept at reading people. It

helped when you had money to know if people were lying to you, and he could tell Carrie wasn't telling the truth. She didn't seem confident enough to be a con artist, and a good one would have had an excuse to get in, but something was off about her. "What sort of business?"

She cleared her throat. "Design, but let's not talk about business. Don't you get enough of that during the day?"

He chuckled. She was adept at changing the subject. "Indeed, I do."

"Great, so let's talk about something else."

"All right, what did you have in mind?" This time he would give her the leash and let her run. He needed to know about her, but direct questions obviously would not get him any answers.

"Oh, I don't know." She glanced around and then finally back at him. A tiny sparkle flashed in her eyes. "What do you do for fun?"

That question caught Drew off guard, and he blinked. What did he do for fun? When he was in college, he had enjoyed the weekly bonfires after football games, and though his mother thought it Neanderthal, he liked watching football games on Sundays, but that was about the extent of it. Work consumed most of his days now. Buying hotels, renovating hotels, hiring employees to work in the hotels. Hotels dominated his life. He enjoyed traveling and seeing new places, but even those trips were often for work and rarely for pleasure which took some of the joy away.

"Don't tell me you don't know how to have fun?" Her head tilted to the side as she looked up at him. For the first time, her voice held a teasing note as if she were finally relaxing around him.

"I know how to have fun; I just don't always have the time for it, I suppose. Though I used to." He sighed as he thought back to his college days when life was simpler. People had known he was wealthy, and the friends he had made came from money as well, but they hadn't talked about it. Money hadn't ruled their life as it seemed to do now. "When I attended college, I was 'free' for a bit. I used to enjoy watching football games and attending the bonfires, actually." He smiled as the memories of those evenings filled his head. The smell of the fire, the relaxed company, the food that neither his cook nor his mother would approve of. "I loved S'mores."

Her lips pulled into a smile. "Really? S'mores? I would have taken you for a more refined dessert eater."

He twirled her around as the music changed. "First off, S'mores are refined. It takes a lot of talent to get the marshmallow toasted just right so it's gooey but not black."

She chuckled, and her smile grew. Her top teeth were straight but one tooth on the bottom turned in slightly. Drew found it endearing. "Granted," she said with a nod. "What's the second reason?"

He pulled her closer and brought his lips to her ear. "I'm not as refined as people think I am."

"Oh, really?"

"Really. I keep my limo stocked with Doritos and beef jerky."

At this she laughed out loud, garnering looks from the

people closest. A pink flush claimed her face, and she snapped her mouth closed. Her eyes dropped to the floor and his heart ached as he watched her wilt. She obviously embarrassed easily.

"Don't worry. They've already forgotten you. So, what about you? What do you do for fun?"

Her posture regained some of its strength, and the corners of her lips twitched. "I love to read and attend church. I especially love the days I get to work in the nursery."

Finally, something he was certain was true about Carrie. He could tell by the tone of her voice. Wistful and honest. He wasn't much of a reader himself, and he was more of a holiday attender than a regular attender at church, but he could relate to the desire to be around children. As an only child, he had no siblings with children, but he liked kids. He wanted kids. He had thought he and Marjorie were headed that direction until she.... Drew shook his head slightly. Marjorie was gone.

"Do you have kids of your own?" he asked Carrie. Not that he was against an instant family, but it changed the dating dynamic. Dating? He was getting ahead of himself. He barely knew this woman, but he could not deny he was attracted to her.

She dropped her eyes and her voice fell flat. "No, I have no kids. Maybe someday."

He touched a finger under her chin and tilted her head up, so she was looking in his eyes. "I have no doubt that some man will sweep you off your feet some day and make that wish come true." As the words came out of his mouth, he found himself wanting to be that guy. What was it about this girl? He rarely found himself enamored so quickly, at least not after Marjorie. She had burned him too badly. Since then, he hadn't met a woman who attracted his interest and managed to hold it this long.

Her teeth bit down on her bottom lip as a sigh raised and lowered her shoulders. "I hope so."

A look of resigned defeat danced across her face, and Drew wondered what was in her past to elicit such emotion? He wanted to fix it, to let her know how beautiful and interesting he found her, but the words in his head sounded hollow, trite. The conversation stalled then, but Drew counted it a victory as her eyes stayed on his. When the song changed, he took her hand and led her to the side of the dance floor. "Are you hungry?"

A small gurgling sound answered his question as Carrie threw her hands over her stomach. "I guess I could eat a little." A sheepish grin played across her face which Drew found endearing. Most of the women he associated with had starved themselves so long, their stomachs never rumbled because they didn't remember the taste of food.

"Come with me then. If I know my mother, she hired the best caterer in town and the food will be delicious though not entirely filling."

"Isn't that always the case at expensive restaurants?" she asked with a laugh though it sounded forced. The charade was back on, the wall back up.

He smiled back at her, but he filed the information away.

Wealthy people rarely referred to restaurants as expensive because, while they might be, it was an expected expense and often a tax write off if done correctly.

The back table was indeed laden with delicacies - canapes, truffles, and more. They grabbed a plate and loaded it with goodies before finding a place to sit. It pleased Drew to see Carrie's plate overflowing with food. He was so tired of women who ate nothing but salad.

"Does your mother always throw such elaborate parties?" Carrie asked as she lifted a canape to her mouth.

Drew noticed her nails for the first time. Or perhaps it was the lack of her nails. Most of the women he'd dated either had fake nails or at the very least had them trimmed and painted. Carrie's nails were devoid of polish and all different lengths. She hadn't seen a manicurist in quite some time. His interest in her grew. Who was this woman?

"Yes," he said dragging his eyes from her hands back to her face. "She does nothing small. Even before my father died, she would throw elaborate parties. I think they might be even bigger now as if she's trying to make up for him being gone or something."

Carrie's smile faltered. "I'm sorry about your father."

"Me too, but he was a good man. I'm glad I had him around as long as I did."

"Yeah, that must be nice." Carrie's voice was so soft that Drew wasn't sure he'd heard her correctly. Her eyes had dropped to her plate.

"Are you close to your family?" he asked.

"I used to be, but no, not anymore."

He wanted to ask her more, but the tone in her voice led him to believe the subject was off limits.

Suddenly, she stiffened. Her eyes widened, and she stood. "I'm sorry, I have to go."

"Wait." He rose as well and grabbed her hand. "I want to see you again. Can I at least have your whole name?"

"No, I'm sorry, I have to go. Thank you for a wonderful evening." She wrestled her hand out of his grip and hurried from the room. Drew stared after her wondering what had just happened. He wasn't used to women running out on him. That was usually his move.

Something sparkly caught his attention. He bent down and picked up a diamond tennis bracelet from the floor. Drew was almost certain it belonged to Carrie. He examined it for some clue of who this mysterious woman was, but the bracelet didn't appear out of the ordinary. It contained no engraving, and while he wasn't a jeweler, he wasn't even sure the diamonds were real. He looked again to the direction she had fled. He had a name, a bracelet, and a partial description. Would it be enough to find her again?

CHAPTER 3

*G*wen didn't stop running until she exited the hotel. She paused just long enough to text Carrie and ask her to send the driver, but the limo hadn't arrived yet. Gwen pressed herself against the building in a shadow to wait. She'd been having such a good time. Why did Grant have to show up and ruin it?

Gwen hadn't seen him enter, but she had been a little distracted. Drew Devonshire was charming. Probably a little too charming as she'd let her guard down. At least until Grant caught her eye as he turned from the buffet table. Gwen just knew he had been coming her direction. Not only would he have ruined it for Carrie, but for Gwen as well. Surely Drew Devonshire would have had her thrown out for crashing his party. At the very least, he probably would have been angry that she lied to him even though it was a tiny lie.

Ugh, this was why she hated lying. It never ended well. No, it had been better just to leave. Unfortunately, as much as she told herself that, it didn't stop her heart from pounding in her chest at the thought of his blue eyes. Nor did it stop her mind from replaying every moment he had held her in his arms while they danced. She'd never felt so attracted to anyone, and she had felt none of the usual anxiety she felt around men. She'd felt like she fit. But of course, he had to be someone completely out of her league who thought she was someone else. Gwen had the worst luck.

She pushed herself off the wall and hurried to the limo when it pulled up to the curb. The driver opened the door for her, and Gwen scrambled inside. As he shut the door, she pressed her face against the darkened windows and peered out, but it appeared neither Grant nor Drew had followed her outside. With a sigh, she leaned back against the seat. It was too bad Grant's appearance had cut the evening short. It was fun while it lasted.

"What happened? Are you all right?" Carrie asked when Gwen arrived at her penthouse twenty minutes later.

Gwen shook her head and dropped her handbag on the table. "I'm fine. The evening was great until Grant showed up. He was making a beeline to talk to me, er, you I guess, and I panicked. I knew he'd know I wasn't you, so I ran."

Carrie's face folded in sympathy. "Oh, Gwen, I'm so sorry. I was hoping you would have a good time."

Gwen plopped onto Carrie's settee and removed her shoes. "I did have a good time. I met the most amazing man, and we danced. He had these arresting blue eyes."

Carrie settled on the settee beside her, and her eyes

sparkled. "Ooh, do tell. Did you catch his name?"

Gwen chuckled and rolled her eyes. "Yeah, Drew Devonshire." Her eyes fell to her lap and she picked off a piece of lint. "Evidently, his family owns the hotel." Gwen lifted her eyes to gauge Carrie's reaction.

Carrie's eyes widened, and her head fell forward. "Drew Devonshire? You danced with Drew Devonshire?"

"Yeah, why? Is he a big deal? I mean I understand he owns the hotel, but-" Gwen reached up to undo her hair. The pins were digging tiny gauges in her head.

Disbelief filled Carrie's voice. "Gwen, Drew Devonshire is only the most eligible billionaire bachelor in the city."

Gwen's hand froze. "What?" How could she have attracted the attention of the most eligible bachelor in the city? She was a nobody. Except that Drew didn't know he'd danced with Gwen Rodgers, lowly teacher. He thought he'd been dancing with some wealthy woman named Carrie.

Carrie chuckled. "Yeah, he doesn't just own *that* hotel, Gwen. His family owns a whole chain."

A sigh escaped Gwen's lips as her hair tumbled about her shoulders. "Figures. I knew he was rich, but I had no idea he was a billionaire." Ugh, embarrassment flooded her. She should never have gone, but at least it had been only the one night. She would never have to see Drew Devonshire again, and he would never have to know.

"You liked him."

"What's not to like? The man is handsome, wealthy, and displayed manners. He was down-to-earth too." Gwen tried to play off her affection, but her heart ached inside.

"No, I mean you *liked* liked him."

Gwen groaned and dropped her head into her hands. "I did, but that's a fantasy, Carrie. He's a billionaire, and I'm a foster kid turned teacher. He would run the other way if he ever knew."

Carrie touched her shoulder. "You don't know that. I'm wealthy and we're still friends."

Gwen lifted her head to look at her friend. "Yeah, but you aren't dating me. You said yourself that one thing you hated about the money was having to live up to the expectations of others. People expect a billionaire like Drew Devonshire to date an heiress or a princess or something. Not someone like me."

Carrie opened her mouth to say something but then closed it again. Gwen knew she had no words either. With a sigh, she pushed herself up. "I'm going to change out of your dress. Guess my Cinderella evening is over."

"I'll pour us a glass of wine while you change," Carrie said as she headed toward the kitchen.

Gwen padded down the hallway to Carrie's bedroom. She slipped out of the dress and pulled her clothes back on. As she hung up the dress, a pang of jealousy coursed through her. It wasn't that she wanted Carrie's life, but it had been nice to pretend. If only for one night. Her hand lingered for a minute on the satin, and then she headed out of the closet to return the earrings to Carrie's dresser. As she put the earrings on the top, her breath caught. She looked at her left wrist and then her right, but both were empty. Where was her bracelet?

Gwen scanned the floor then retraced her steps in the closet. Nothing. No, this couldn't be happening. She couldn't lose the last thing her parents had given her. "No, no, no," she mumbled under her breath as she cleared the closet and headed down the hall. Her heart wound tighter as she walked as if squeezed by an invisible vice, and she felt the tears building behind her eyes.

"What's the matter?" Carrie asked as Gwen entered the kitchen.

Gwen looked up, tears blurring her vision. "I can't find my bracelet." With those five words, the dam broke and the tears spilled down her cheeks. "I think I lost it."

Carrie's eyes grew large and she sucked in her breath. "I'll call Antwon and see if it got left in the limo. He's good people, Gwen, he wouldn't have taken it."

"But what if I lost it at the Devonshire Hotel? I'll never find it again."

Carrie wrapped an arm about Gwen's shoulder. "It will be okay. I promise we will find it."

Gwen's knees gave out and she sank to the floor. "It's all I have left of them, Carrie."

"I know, and it will be okay. I promise."

But Gwen wasn't so sure.

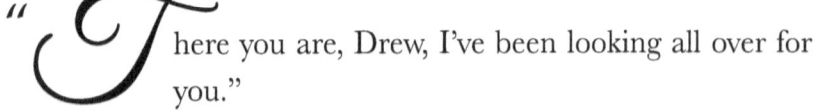

"There you are, Drew, I've been looking all over for you."

Drew turned to see his mother, dressed as Queen Elizabeth and wearing a fancy mask, heading his direction.

"Where have you been?"

He ignored her question and posed his own as his hand closed over the bracelet, hiding the contents from sight. "Is there a guest list?"

The question seemed to fluster his mother. "Is there what? What are you talking about Drew? I asked where you've been."

"I've been here, Mother, dancing with an amazing woman, but she ran off and dropped her bracelet. I'd like to return it to her. So, I'll ask you again. Is there a guest list?"

His mother puffed up. "Of course, there is a guest list. This party was by invitation only, but why don't you just deliver it?"

"Because I didn't get her full name, Mother. It's a masquerade ball, and she was playing coy."

"Well, what about her bracelet? Is it engraved at all?"

Drew unfurled his hand to show his mother the bracelet. "No engraving."

His mother picked up the bracelet and examined it. Her forehead furrowed behind her mask and disdain dripped from her voice when she responded, "This isn't even real, Drew. These are fake diamonds. This woman was probably an imposter."

"Perhaps, but she was intriguing and imposter or not, I want to return her bracelet. It might be nothing to us, but I have the feeling it was to her. Why else would a woman wear a designer dress and a fake bracelet?"

His mother rolled her eyes. "I can think of many reasons. I'll get you the guest list but promise me you won't waste your time chasing after some ghost."

Drew couldn't promise, but he nodded hoping it would satisfy his mother.

She let out a large sigh. "Fine, come with me."

He followed her out the ballroom and down the hall to her office. The namesake hotel was the one she liked to work out of most days. She said she felt the strongest connection to it since his father had purchased it first before Drew even was born.

She pushed open the office door after producing a key from some fold in her dress. After a minute of scanning the papers on the desk, she picked up a large stack and held it out to him. "Here you are." Without another word, she whizzed past him and left the room.

Drew took the stack of papers to the desk and sat down. He grabbed a pen from his mother's container and began scanning the list.

Fifteen minutes later, Drew sighed as he finished the last page of the guest list. It appeared his mother invited everyone in the Tristate area. A dozen Carries filled his list that he would have to check and that was only if she'd given him the right first name. Drew wasn't even sure of that. Finding this woman might be like finding a needle in a haystack, but he would try. He didn't even know why it was so important, other than she was the first woman who had excited him in a long time.

CHAPTER 4

*D*rew typed in the next name on the list. It had taken him a few days to find the time to search the Carries on the list, but determination pushed him to find the woman from the ball. Carrie Garner. An older brunette woman popped up on the screen. Real estate mogul. Nope, not the right one. That just left one more name. Carrie Bliss. He typed it into the search bar and a dress designer's website pulled up, but there was no picture. Great. He added her to the list of other no picture Carries. At least this list was smaller. Only three names. Down from twelve. Drew glanced over at the diamond tennis bracelet. He wasn't optimistic, but maybe his jeweler could help.

He shut the laptop screen and pocketed the bracelet before pulling out his cell phone. "Manuel? Can you have the limo ready in five? Wonderful, I'll be right down." Drew flicked his wrist to read the time on his Rolex. He had a few hours to spare. Enough time to see his jeweler before the auction tonight if he hurried.

With a hastened step, he crossed to his closet and pulled out his blue dress shirt. Women always told him it made his blue eyes pop, and though he wasn't looking for a woman tonight, he wouldn't mind the confidence booster. His mother had insisted he attend a charity auction with her.

He tucked the shirt into his black slacks and shrugged into an Armani blazer. Tie or no tie? Drew regarded his appearance in the mirror. He hated ties. They always made him feel as if he was choking, but his mother nagged him when he didn't wear one. No. No tie. He might have to attend this event, but at least he could be comfortable during it.

Being the public face had never been Drew's strength. That's where his father had excelled and so when he passed, his mother assumed Drew would too, but he hated it. Maybe if he was married, it would be different, but being single and wealthy, it just made him feel like a piece of meat at the market. Men would eye him like competition and women would scan him from head to toe. It was even worse after Marjorie left as he was never sure if those stares were of interest or pity. Either way, they made Drew uncomfortable, and one day he hoped to pass the job off to someone else.

He trotted down the grand staircase and out the front door. Manuel was just pulling in front of the house as Drew shut the door behind him. Drew folded himself into the spacious backseat when Manuel held the door open.

"Where to, sir?"

Drew fingered the bracelet in his pocket. "To Barelli's, Manuel."

Joseph Barelli had been his father's jeweler before Drew was even born. He was a wealthy Italian a few years older than Drew's father would have been. Though his hair was grey, the man was still extremely handsome and always immaculately dressed. Drew figured it had to be some magic gene Italians were born with.

"Ah, what can I do for you today, Seignior Devonshire?" Mr. Barelli asked when Drew entered the shop.

"I need to see if you can tell me anything about a bracelet." Drew withdrew the bracelet from his pocket and handed it to the elder gentleman.

"Mm, let me see." Mr. Barelli grabbed a magnifying tool from the counter behind him and perused the bracelet. His brows knitted together in confusion as he turned the bracelet in his hand. "I don't know what you are hoping for, sir, but this is an ordinary tennis bracelet."

Drew sighed. "I figured as much. Are there no distinguishing features?"

Mr. Barelli shook his head. "It is not even high quality. This could have been sold at any discount store in the country. May I ask why you are so curious about it?"

"A woman who attended my mother's masquerade ball the other night dropped it."

Mr. Barelli blinked at Drew. "Why would someone of your mother's status be wearing such a trinket?"

"That seems to be the million-dollar question, my friend," Drew said with a smile. "This woman was intriguing, but very different from Mother's normal guests."

"Well, I wish you the best of luck in finding the owner, and please, let me know how the story ends."

"I will, if I ever find her again." Drew took the bracelet back and stared at it for just a moment before returning it to his pocket. "Thank you again."

"No luck, sir?" Manuel asked as Drew slid into the back of the limo.

"No. Just a trinket as I suspected. The good news is the list is smaller now, so I'll check out the few remaining women tomorrow. Tonight, however, I have to get to the auction."

"I admire what you are doing, sir," Manuel said as he started the limo. "Not everyone would display such commitment."

Drew nodded and leaned back against the seat. It was true. Most people in his position would not have gone searching for the owner of the bracelet. He wasn't even sure why he was doing it, other than some urge compelled him. No, not just an urge. It was something else. Something in the woman's bright green eyes or the way she felt in his arms. It was something different that he hadn't even realized he was missing until it was gone.

wen sighed and tried one last time to twist her unruly red curls into some semblance of an up do. Her boss was particular that no tendrils hung down

while she was serving food, but the Irish in her blood made pinning them down almost impossible.

She squeezed a tiny bit of gel into her hands and rubbed them together. Then she wiped her hands across her hair. The gel managed to tame the last few locks into place. Of course, Gwen had no idea if it would last all night, but at least it was a start.

After a final look in the mirror, she decided her appearance would suffice, flicked off the light, and wandered into the living room to grab her purse.

Carrie looked up from the couch where she sat playing with Tabby. Tabby was Gwen's kitten - her one financial splurge because she had been so lonely. Carrie had offered to cat sit Tabby while Gwen worked her second job as a caterer. She didn't want the responsibility of a pet full time, but Carrie loved coming over and having play time with Tabby while Gwen catered.

"Where are you off to tonight?" Carrie asked as she tucked a lock of hair behind her ear. Gwen tried not to envy Carrie's hair. Though also a ginger, God had blessed her with hair that followed directions, and it lay on her shoulders like velvety copper.

"Who knows? I never know till I get there." Gwen didn't love catering, but her teaching job was barely earning enough to pay the bills. Every paycheck went directly to her student loan, rent, cell phone, groceries, and her car. It was enough to get by but not enough to start saving, so Gwen had picked up a second job catering on the weekends.

Carrie wrinkled her perfect ski-sloped nose, and Gwen

swallowed another tiny seed of jealousy. Carrie was feminine perfection. Small nose, delicate lips, slender hands. Gwen, on the other hand, wasn't. Her nose was too big and dusted with freckles, her lips were too thin, and her feet were a size ten - too large to be considered delicate. In fact, her last boyfriend had called them Hobbit feet. She didn't miss that aspect of him.

"Ugh, I'm sorry. I don't know how you work around food all night. I'd either be eating it all or vomiting from the smells."

Gwen rolled her eyes. Carrie rarely ate more than a salad and chicken breast. There was no way she would put the greasy half-baked half-fried food that Gwen served in her mouth. Of course, that was probably why Carrie was a size six while Gwen struggled to maintain her thicker size eight to ten.

"Well, we don't get to eat the food often, and puking on the job is frowned upon." However, it wasn't always easy. She didn't like most of the food she served, but the London Broil was fabulous. Occasionally, when there was food left over, the caterers could eat after they cleaned up. It wasn't always warm by then, but the London Broil even heated well.

"What do you think it is tonight? A wedding?"

Gwen shook her head as she grabbed her coat and scarf. "No, wrong time of year for a wedding. Birthday party maybe or some work thing." Gwen was generally more upbeat, but the loss of her bracelet plus her landlord raising her rent had her down. People said God never gave you more than you could handle, but Gwen felt at the end of her rope.

"I know it's hard right now, but if you ever need money, all you have to do is ask," Carrie said.

Gwen sighed. "I know, but you know I want to take care of myself as long as I can." She'd had to depend on people too long in foster care, and things hadn't always turned out in her favor. When she reached the age of eighteen, Gwen made a promise to herself that she would be self-sufficient. She hoped she wouldn't have to break it. "Take care of my fur ball," she said as she pulled open the front door and headed into the parking lot.

Ten minutes later, Gwen pulled into the parking lot of the catering company. She grabbed her green apron from the passenger seat and stuffed it in her purse before exiting the car and locking the door. She didn't mind the work, but the uniform left a lot to be desired. Black pants, white shirt, and the ugly forest green apron.

Her co-worker, Rachel, was already hard at work grabbing items from the list and stuffing them in the bins. In addition to the food, they had to bring enough plates, bowls, cups, and silverware along with serving utensils and the Sterno containers to heat the food. Someone cooked most of the food the night before and then wrapped it up and placed in the refrigerator.

"What can I help with?" Gwen asked as she tossed her purse on the table. She grabbed her apron from it and tied it about her waist.

"I'm packing the serving utensils. Do you want to grab the plates and bowls?"

"Sure." Rachel handed over the list and Gwen scanned the numbers. This would not be a large party. Probably not a birthday party then. Small parties meant fewer dishes, but it meant serving people at the table instead of in a buffet line. It was a good thing Gwen had worn her comfortable shoes. She'd be earning her ten thousand steps tonight.

Gwen grabbed a tub and began loading the plates in. They were in the cabinet in sets of tens, so she placed five rows in the tub. Then she filled in the remaining space with the bowls packing them carefully to avoid breakage. By the time she finished, Rachel had packed the utensils and moved on to checking the food.

"Who's working with us today?" Gwen asked. Fifty people wasn't too large for two, but it would be easier with three.

Rachel rolled her eyes. "Martin, but you know how he is. It might as well be just you and me."

Martin was their boss. At only twenty-three, he was younger than them both, but he was the manager because his family owned the catering company. Gwen hated nepotism, especially when it allowed inept people to be in positions of power. Martin was such a person. He didn't think he needed to do the prep work or the clean-up work. He would show up just in time to drive the truck. Then he would disappear when it came time to unload until everything was set up. Even during the serving, he would spend more time chatting with the patrons than serving people.

Gwen sighed. It would be a long night, but at least the pay would be worth it. Hopefully, she would earn enough to sock some away in her savings. Her apartment was fine, but she wanted a home of her own - something she hadn't had since the age of twelve when her parents died. She had been putting a little from every catering job in savings, and she hoped to put a down payment on a little house soon.

Gwen joined Rachel in loading the food, and after a second check, they began carting the tubs out to the van. As the last tub slid in, Martin appeared.

"Oh, good, it looks like you two are ready. Sorry, I was caught in a phone call."

Gwen and Rachel traded looks. Martin was always caught in something. It was called an aversion to work.

"Well, let's load up." As expected, Martin climbed into the driver's side. Gwen slid into the middle, and Rachel followed suit, sitting closest to the door. The ride was quiet and uncomfortable. Gwen couldn't wait until they arrived, and she could focus on work.

A few minutes later, Martin pulled up in front of the back entrance of the hall where the event was being held. "I'll park here while you girls unload, and then I'll be in to help set up."

Rachel let out a soft snort. They both knew that wouldn't happen. She opened her door and held it open for Gwen to scoot out as well. When it was shut, they walked to the back of the van to begin unloading.

"At least we can do it all in one trip," Rachel said with a sigh as she eyed the tubs.

"Just tell yourself it's your workout." Gwen tried to hit the gym a few times a week after work, but she knew she needed to lift more. Her clothes always fit a little better when she did.

"Yeah, if only I liked working out." Rachel was larger than Gwen, short and stocky. Though Gwen didn't know her well, Rachel often spoke of cooking as her hobby. Gwen thought she had mentioned wanting to author a cookbook once.

They pulled down the first cart and hefted one of the tubs onto the bottom shelf. Then they climbed back in the van to grab a second tub for the top shelf.

"You'd think he could help while he's parked here," Rachel hissed under her breath.

Gwen shrugged. She didn't like it either, but she wasn't one to buck authority. She needed the job too much, and she'd never had the courage to stand up to people. When her parents had been killed, she'd gone into the foster system. Some foster kids bucked the system and revolted, but Gwen had gone the other direction - retreating into her shell. Her first home had been awful, but when the CPS worker had finally checked on her and found her locked in a closet, she'd been removed. The next place had been much better. Those foster parents had been nice, but Gwen had never really let them in. Losing people hurt too much, and trust was hard for her to give.

With the first cart full, Gwen helped Rachel load the

other cart, and they wheeled them into the building. The kitchen was large and uncluttered which Gwen was thankful for. She hated when there was no kitchen and they had to bring back the dishes to wash them. By then, caked on food made it harder to scrub off, and they invariably had to wash the tub as well.

Rachel checked her watch. "Well, we have about an hour, so I guess we should get set up. We can wait to start the Sterno for another few minutes."

Gwen nodded and opened her tub.

CHAPTER 5

The limo stopped in front of the small building. "Here we are, sir," Manuel said from the driver's seat as he turned off the engine.

Drew waited for Manuel to open the door before stepping out. His eyes scanned the building as he stood. Not large, but a nice location nonetheless. The hall sat on the edge of a river, and one wall was entirely glass, granting an astounding view of the area.

"Thank you, Manuel. Keep your phone on in case I can sneak out of here early."

Manuel nodded. "As you wish, sir."

Drew returned the nod and ran a hand down his suit before heading into the building. A man in black pants and a crisp white shirt opened the door. Drew hadn't been expecting a doorman at such a small event. He motioned to the closed doors straight ahead. "Enjoy your night, sir."

If only he could, but Drew had been attending these

events for so long that the novelty had worn off. There had been a time he once loved dressing up in a suit and attending the affairs. They had made him feel important, something he didn't always feel knowing his money wasn't his but an inheritance from his father. In addition, he had harbored the notion he would meet his future wife at one of these events.

However, the women were much like the food - they all looked the same after the first few events. Sure, they showed up in their designer dresses looking like a million dollars. They smiled at all the right times and laughed at his jokes, but on the very next date, their true colors emerged. The smile was a little tighter, the questions a little more personal, and he could almost feel their fingers reaching into his bank account to spend his money. He didn't want a woman like that.

Drew took one final deep breath, plastered his fake smile on, and opened the door. The room held ten round tables focused on a podium at the front. Most of the tables were already full. He glanced around for a waiter or a bar but found neither. Drew wasn't much of a drinker, but nights like this he needed one.

His discomfort grew when he heard the shrill voice of his mother beckoning him from across the room. "Drew, over here, darling." She waved at him from across the room. At nearly sixty, his mother was still in great shape. Of course, she paid good money to have a cook and a personal trainer, but he wished she wouldn't draw such attention to herself or him.

Shaking his head, he made his way across the floor to her

table. He gave her the obligatory peck on each cheek before addressing her. "Mother, I wish you wouldn't yell like that across the room. I abhor these things as it is, but I especially detest when you make a scene."

His mother folded her arms and leaned back as she regarded him. "I brought you into this world, Drew Devonshire. Need I remind you of my twelve-hour labor?"

Drew rolled his eyes. This was always the card she played when he brought up anything she disagreed with. As if he controlled how long she was in labor. "No, you needn't, but, Mother, really. I would have made my way over to you, eventually."

"Perhaps," she said, tilting her head, "but I needed you here sooner rather than later."

His heart sank as her eyes twinkled. "Oh, no, Mother, what did you do?" He knew that look in her eye, and he rarely liked it.

She held out her thin, perfectly manicured hands. "I did nothing. I happened to meet a lovely woman earlier. She's new to these charity events, but it turns out she has a daughter just about your age."

Drew groaned. "Tell me you didn't." His mother was always setting him up with one wealthy debutante after another even though he'd told her they were too vanilla, too boring for him.

"Relax, I just said they should sit with us. The rest is up to you. Oh, here they are now. Camilla, over here, darling." Her arm waved in the air again and Drew stifled his sigh. This was what he hated more than the stuffy event itself, this awkward moment when he met someone his mother was clearly trying to set him up with and had to play nice, no matter what she looked like or what strange habits she had.

The last time his mother had done this, the woman had been obsessed with her weight. Even though she had been tiny, she had tugged on Drew's arm every few minutes asking how many calories were in that canape or would that drink cause her hips to grow? He couldn't get away from her fast enough.

The time before that, the woman had seemed normal enough at first. Then, she had proceeded to pull a tiny compact out of her bag to check her appearance. Not unordinary for women, but the compact had then disappeared and reappeared ten times in the span of five minutes. Who needed to look at themselves that often? Needless to say, Drew was not a fan of these set ups, so he was pleasantly surprised when he turned around.

"Avery?" Though he hadn't seen her in years, he was sure it was Avery. This woman was small and petite with her brown hair piled on her head. Her silver gown hugged her frame, and her blue eyes sparkled.

"Drew?" There was a hint of laughter in her voice as she answered.

His mother blinked in confusion. "You two know each other?"

Drew chuckled. He and Avery had dated a few years ago. She was one of the few wealthy women he had met who held his interest, but before they grew serious, she had moved away. "Yes, we know each other. You look beautiful, Avery."

"You clean up pretty nice yourself," she said as she placed her hands on her hips and looked him up and down.

"Well, I guess there's no need to introduce the two of you." His mother turned her attention to Avery's mother. "Camilla, I'm so glad you could make it. This is my son Drew."

Camilla was an older version of her daughter. Grey streaks ran through her hair and the lines around her eyes were more pronounced, but she appeared to take good care of herself. "Pleased to meet you, Drew," she said as she extended her hand to him. "Though I'm surprised I haven't met you before if you know Avery."

Drew took the woman's hand. Soft, but slightly leathery. "A pleasure to meet you as well." His eyes shifted to Avery. "Well, Avery and I knew each other a few years ago, but then she moved away. Are you back now?"

Avery returned the smile, but it didn't reach her eyes. "Yes, apparently I am." There was a sadness in her voice that he didn't remember. What had happened to her? When her mother looked away though, Drew caught Avery's eye roll and bit back a smile. Maybe this evening wouldn't be so bad after all.

❀

"It's showtime, ladies," Martin said. "I'll stay back here and get the plates ready as you two serve."

Rachel rolled her eyes, but Gwen spoke up. "Sure, Martin, that sounds good." She picked up two plates and headed for the swinging door that connected the kitchen to the hall. The tables were now full, and a dull hum of conversation filled the air.

Gwen fixed a smile on her face as she approached the first table. Interacting with the guests was her least favorite part of catering, but it came with the territory. At least at events like this, the men and women rarely spoke to her. They were too engaged in their own conversations and conversing with "the help" was beneath them.

She placed a plate in front of the first woman who didn't even bother to look her direction and then one in front of the man next to her. He flicked her a passing glance, but that was all. Gwen returned to the kitchen and grabbed two more plates.

Rachel had taken the other half of the room. Five tables apiece was still a lot, but it was manageable. Gwen placed the next two plates down and returned to the kitchen one more time. She repeated this procedure until only one table remained. As she approached the final table though her eyes widened. No, it couldn't be.

Only two men sat at this table. One was an elderly gentleman with a round face and a receding hairline. The other was a dashing young man with dark hair and blue eyes. He looked remarkably like Drew Devonshire. It was true she had only glimpsed his face that night when he lifted his mask, but those blue eyes were seared in her memory. Her heart sped up in her chest.

Unfortunately, he wasn't alone. A stunning brunette sat to his right, and from the smile on her face, she appeared as smitten as Gwen felt. She looked around for Rachel. Was it too late to trade tables? She wasn't sure she could work this one all night. What if he recognized her? Or maybe worse, what if he didn't?

Rachel was just placing a plate down at her final table. Too late to switch now. Gwen would just have to hope he ignored her like the others had or that he wouldn't recognize her without the mask. She kept her head turned slightly away from him as she placed her two plates and then made a beeline for the kitchen.

Her face felt flushed as she exited the hall and entered the kitchen. She needed to cool down. If she went back out with a bright red face, she would just draw more attention to herself. Gwen closed her eyes and leaned against the wall trying to calm her heart down.

"Grab a tray and take the last three," Martin ordered when he spotted her. "I'm about ready to start sending out the next course."

Gwen wanted to say no, to come up with some excuse, but she needed this job. She took a deep breath and grabbed the tray. Hoping her face had calmed down, Gwen headed back into the hall. *Please don't look at me. Please don't look at me.* The mantra played over and over in her head as she approached his table.

She placed the plate in front of the older woman first and then turned to Drew. Thankfully, his face was turned toward his brunette friend. She scooted his plate in front of him and then delivered the plate to the brunette. Her heartbeat thundered in her ears. How could they not hear it? Drew's eyes lifted to hers, and Gwen sucked in her breath.

"Thank you," he said and then turned back to his friend.

"You're welcome," Gwen stuttered. She was too shocked to say anything else. He hadn't recognized her. She should be happy, but disbelief was all she could feel right now.

With a sigh, she headed back to the kitchen. One course down and only two more to go.

CHAPTER 6

*D*rew raised his hand to cover his mouth as the second yawn struck him. He'd managed to stifle the first, but the second had snuck up on him.

"Are you as bored as I am?" Avery asked as she leaned in close to him.

"Maybe more." He smiled at her. She was the first wealthy woman he'd met who seemed to hate these events as much as he did. It was one reason they had tried dating years ago. He glanced at his watch. They still had another few hours. They had served the first course along with the main course, but dessert remained, and bidding would probably start during dessert.

"You think we could sneak out during dessert?" he whispered back.

Her blue eyes sparkled. "You mean skip the auction? You bet I do, but only if it isn't a date. No offense, but we tried that once already."

"Yes, but that didn't work out because you left."

"No, that didn't work out because you're exactly what my mother wants me to marry. I don't want to marry what my mother wants. I want to marry what I want, and that does not include billionaires who would drag me to stuffy events like this."

Drew chuckled. He liked Avery, he missed her quick wit, and it was true. Their romance had fizzled before she left though he couldn't really remember why. However, he had enjoyed their friendship, and if she was back in town, he wanted to rekindle it. "Okay, not a date then. I kind of have another woman on my mind anyway."

Avery flashed him a crooked smile and leaned closer. "Ooh, do tell."

"I met her at my mother's masquerade ball the other night. She was beautiful, but she didn't act like she knew it."

Avery chuckled. "How was she at your mother's ball then?"

"I'm not sure she was supposed to be." He moved his arm as the server approached. "She certainly didn't act like the other rich women my mother is always trying to set me up with, but she said she was on the list." The plate clattered against the table and Drew looked up at the woman. Her face was pale, and her eyes were wide, but there was something familiar in them.

"I'm so sorry," she said averting her eyes.

Her voice tickled his ears and triggered a memory, but it couldn't be. She'd said she owned her own business, so why would she be serving at an auction?

Fear flickered in her eyes, and her eyes glanced around for the nearest exit. In that instant he knew. "It is you."

"I'm sorry," she mumbled again and ran for the side door. He wasn't letting her get away this time though.

"What's going on?" his mother asked.

"Nothing. I'll be right back." Drew tossed his napkin on the table and hurried after the woman. He didn't even care that he was causing a scene behind him.

As he pushed open the door, he found her leaning against the wall to his left. When she heard the door open, she looked up and turned to bolt.

"Carrie, wait."

She stopped in her tracks and though her back was to him, he saw her shoulders droop. Slowly, she turned to face him. "My name isn't Carrie."

"What do you mean?" He took a step toward her aware that he should be increasing the distance between them after her admission instead of closing it.

"My friend is Carrie Bliss, the dress designer your mother invited. She asked me to attend in her place. I'm sorry. I didn't know I would meet you, and I didn't think I was hurting anyone."

"You didn't," he said taking another step. "I'm glad you were there for whatever reason. Those parties generally bore me to no end, but you… you made it interesting."

She stared at him, her green eyes peering into his soul. "Why?"

He blinked, her question catching him off guard. "I don't know why. Maybe because you were genuine."

She raised her eyebrow at him, and he chuckled as the irony of his statement sunk in.

"Okay, other than the fake name part. I felt there were parts of you that were genuine like when you talked about working in the nursery. I'm surrounded by so many people that only say what they think I want to hear. You didn't seem to care about that. It was refreshing."

"Well, I'm glad. Look, I'm probably going to get fired when my boss finds out I caused a scene, but I should really get back to work."

"Wait." He reached into his pocket and pulled out the bracelet. He'd been carrying it with him everywhere since the night of the ball as if he hoped it might help him find her again. As he held it out to her, it surprised him to see her eyes glisten with tears. "It's important to you then?"

She nodded, taking the bracelet from his palm. "It's the last thing my parents gave me before someone killed them. It's all I have left, and I thought I'd lost it for good. Thank you."

"You're welcome." He should leave it at that. Say 'you're welcome' and walk away. His mother would never approve of him seeing someone like this woman, whatever her name was, but he couldn't make his feet move away from her. They were rooted in place, glued to the floor. He'd felt something when he danced with her that he'd never felt, and he wanted to feel it again. "Will you tell me your real name now?"

She chuckled and shook her head. "It's Gwen. Gwen Rodgers."

"Well, Gwen Rodgers, I would really like to see you again. Do you think we could arrange that?"

Her eyes lit up for a moment and then the light flickered and faded. Sadness laced her voice as she answered. "No, I don't think that would be a good idea. We come from two different worlds, Drew. Thank you for returning the bracelet, but I have to be going."

Stunned, he watched her walk away. He should be relieved because she was right of course. They did come from different worlds, and his mother would never approve, but that didn't erase the tug of curiosity he was feeling.

The door behind him opened and Avery's head appeared. "You better get back here. Your mother is livid, and she wants an explanation."

With a sigh, Drew followed Avery back to the table.

"What is going on, Drew?" his mother asked. "You have caused quite a scene in here. The looks have been downright scandalous, and you know very well there will be talk tomorrow."

"I'm sorry, Mother. That was the woman from the dance the other night. I wanted to give her back her bracelet."

"You carried it around with you?" His mother's forehead wrinkled, and her nose turned up in disgust. "You better not be falling for this girl, Drew."

*G*wen waited until she was around the corner and out of sight of Drew to let the tears fall. She was thankful to have her bracelet back, embarrassed at the scene she had caused, and angry or disappointed - she wasn't sure which - that she had turned him down. Gwen knew she had made the right decision - telling him they were too different - but a part of her wished she had said yes. She hadn't felt a connection like that with anyone, ever.

She opened her hand and stared down at the bracelet. It looked so ordinary compared to the jewelry the women were wearing out there, but it meant the world to her. With a shaky hand, she fastened it around her wrist once more and then continued to the kitchen.

"Where have you been?" Martin asked. "Rachel has already started bringing back her dishes."

"Sorry, I uh had to take a short break. I'll get right back out there."

"No, you stay here and start washing. *I'll* bring your dishes back." Martin emphasized the word to let her know she was causing him extra trouble. Then he shot her an agitated look before exiting through the swinging door.

Gwen bit back a smile. He thought he was punishing her, but she'd rather be holed up back here than face Drew and his party again. She rolled up her sleeves and filled the sink with water.

"You gonna tell me what happened out there?" Rachel asked as she placed another round of dishes on the counter.

Gwen kept her head down and focused on scrubbing.

Maybe if she feigned ignorance Rachel would let it go. "I don't know what you mean."

Rachel scoffed. "Yes, you do. Some handsome, wealthy man left his entire table to follow you. The whole room saw it."

Gwen bit her lip and sighed. Nope, ignorance was clearly out of the question. "Okay." She turned off the water and glanced toward the door to make sure Martin wasn't around. "I met Drew Devonshire at a masquerade ball the other night."

"You were invited to a ball that Drew Devonshire attended?" Rachel's words were slow and incredulous.

"No, not me, my friend, Carrie. She didn't want to go, and we look similar, so she asked me to go as her. I didn't know it was an elite ball. Anyway, I lost my bracelet and when Drew recognized me tonight, he followed me out to return it."

Rachel narrowed her eyes. "That's it? He followed you out to return it?"

Gwen shrugged. "And to tell me he wanted to see me again, but I said no," she added quickly.

Rachel's eyes bulged, and her jaw dropped. "You said what? Girl, have you lost your mind? Drew Devonshire wants to see you again and you said no?"

"It would never work out. He's... well, he's Drew Devonshire, and I'm... no one."

"Girl, that's why you say yes. Don't you remember Cinderella? Pretty Woman? They were nobodies too, but rich men fell for them and their whole lives changed."

Rachel shook her head as if she couldn't believe Gwen could be so dense.

"Yeah, but those were fairy tales, Rachel. This is reality, and *that* just doesn't happen in reality."

"Guess you'll never know now." Rachel shot her one last disbelieving look before exiting the swinging door.

Gwen stared after her. Was she right? Had Gwen passed up a chance to be a real-life Cinderella? She shook her head. No. She believed in God and she believed in miracles, but that just seemed too farfetched to be true.

CHAPTER 7

*D*rew woke up the next morning determined to learn all he could about Gwen Rodgers. He kicked off the heavy comforter and padded to his desk where his laptop sat. He started with a simple search for her online. It was rare nowadays for people to have no online presence. There was usually a social media page or three, videos and pictures that others had posted, and sometimes even an address. Gwen had none of these. In fact, the only thing he could find was her school picture.

So, she was a teacher as well. A noble profession. And she must not have a lot of money if she was working two jobs. But this wasn't the information he sought. He wanted to determine if she was married and what her interests were. He wanted to know her. It was time to call in a favor.

He picked up the phone next to his computer and rang Manuel. "Can you have the car ready in fifteen? I need to go downtown."

"Of course, sir. It will be waiting for you."

"Thank you." Drew hung up and shut the laptop lid. He needed a quick shower and something to eat and there was no time to waste.

Ten minutes later, clean and dressed, Drew headed down to the kitchen to grab a breakfast on the go. Usually, he let his master chef, Ernesto, whip him up a healthy fare, but there was no time today.

"Good morning, Mr. Devonshire," Ernesto said in greeting as he entered the kitchen. "Egg white omelet today?"

"No time, Ernesto. Must see about a girl. I'll just take a bar with me."

Ernesto's lips pulled into a grimace and his nose rose in the air. "If you had let me know, sir, I could have had breakfast waiting. You needn't have resorted to a processed bar."

Drew smiled. "I suppose that's true. Tell you what, Ernesto, if I'm back in time for lunch, I'll let you serve whatever you feel like making, okay?"

A tiny light of enthusiasm sparked in Ernesto's eyes, but he was too composed to show much more than that. "I await your word."

Drew nodded, ducked into the pantry and grabbed the forbidden bar, and then headed to the front door. Manuel was indeed waiting for him. He leaned against the limo but straightened as soon as he saw Drew.

"Good morning, sir."

"Morning, Manuel. I need to go to the police station downtown."

If Manuel wondered why, he said nothing, just nodded and opened the door for Drew.

Twenty minutes later, the limo pulled to a stop in front of the police station. Drew waited for Manuel to open the door before stepping out and taking in the short brick building. How Scott worked in this bland building every day was beyond him. He must really love his job.

Scott was the one college friend Drew kept in touch with. It never hurt to have someone on the force in your corner. Drew had never had to ask for a favor, but he hoped that his annual donation would be enough to buy him one today.

"Drew Devonshire?" Scott's voice carried across the small room as Drew entered. Several other heads swiveled his direction as he crossed the room to his friend. "Well, I never thought I'd see you in here." Scott shook Drew's hand and motioned at an empty chair.

Drew cleared his throat. "Actually, is there a private room in which we can converse?"

Scott's eyebrow arched, but he led the way down the hall to a conference room. When the door was shut, he turned to Drew. "Okay, you want to tell me what's going on?"

"I was hoping you could find out some information on someone for me."

"Someone who owes you money?"

Drew chuckled. "Hardly. I doubt this person has much."

"So, someone you are hoping to buy out?" Scott was clearly fishing.

"No, a woman I met. She's like no one I've met before; she won't even let me take her to dinner. I tried to gather information about her online, but she doesn't even have a social media page. Who doesn't have a social media platform nowadays?"

This time Scott smiled. "More people than you'd think but continue."

"She's a teacher at Ryland High. That's all I know, but that means she'll be in the system, right? You can find something out about her?"

"Her fingerprints will be in the system, yes. It doesn't mean I'll be able to find out much about her. If she's a teacher, I doubt she has a record."

"Please, whatever you can find."

*G*wen was just finishing prepping for her final lesson of the day when Carol, the school secretary, popped her head in her doorway. "Gwen, you got a second?"

"Sure, Carol, what's up?"

Carol laughed. "How about you tell me? These just came for you." She stepped the rest of the way into the room, and Gwen's eyes widened. In her hands was an enormous bouquet of white carnations and stargazer lilies. "It seems you have an admirer."

A soft heat crawled up Gwen's neck. She assumed they were from Drew, but she didn't want to accept them. After finishing the dishes and packing up the night before, Martin had informed her that she was fired. Evidently, someone at Drew's table had complained about her causing a scene. Rachel had tried to stick up for her, but it was no use. Now, in addition to everything else, she needed to find another part-time job. However, that was way more than she was prepared to share with Carol. She would graciously accept the flowers and get rid of them later when no one would notice.

"Thank you." Gwen took the flowers and looked around for an empty counter to set them on. Her desk was out of the question. She was what most people referred to as "organized chaos." Papers cluttered her desk, and while no one else knew where anything was, Gwen could always find anything needed. She figured it was an unconscious rebelling from living with her mother.

Gwen and her mother had been polar opposites. Her mother was a complete neat nick while Gwen thrived with a little clutter. She always hated Saturdays when her mother made her dust the furniture, vacuum the house, and clean her room. At least, she hated them until her mother died. Then Gwen regretted ever fighting with her mother, and she had bargained with God to never complain about cleaning if he just brought her parents back. Of course, that hadn't happened, and Gwen had retreated into her shell. But as much as she tried to be like her mother, she just couldn't be as organized as her mother had been.

Her file cabinet was about the only furniture in her room clean enough and large enough to hold the flowers, so she set them there. They filled the space looking more like a small garden in her room than a bouquet. A white card sat nestled in a plastic contraption that looked a little like a tuning fork. Though she wasn't sure she cared what the note said, Gwen plucked it out and opened the card.

"It was such a pleasure to meet you, Gwen. I know you think we are worlds apart, but there is more to me than the money. My hope is you will enjoy these flowers and give me another chance. I have included my number, so you can reach out to me, and I await your call." - *Drew*

His number was indeed at the bottom, but there was no apology. Did he not know she had gotten fired? Gwen bit her lip as she contemplated rushing to her phone and calling him right then though she wasn't sure 'thank you' would be the words out of her mouth.

"So?"

Gwen looked up surprised to still see Carol standing in her room, "Oh, just a thank you for someone I met the other night."

Carol's brow shot up. "Wow, that must've been some meeting."

It really had been, and Gwen wasn't even sure why. They had just danced and talked, but there was something in the way he had held her that made her feel safe and secure. Something she hadn't felt in a long time.

But she didn't want to share this with Carol. For one thing, she really couldn't even explain it. For another, she feared if she talked about it, the night would feel less real, less special somehow. And there was the firing thing. So instead, she feigned nonchalance. "I guess it was."

Carol stood a moment longer as if expecting more, but she finally shrugged. "All right, well, I look forward to the story one day. Enjoy your flowers."

Gwen wasn't certain she could do that. Were these apology flowers? If so, was he so arrogant he thought he didn't need the actual apology? She hadn't thought he was. So, maybe he didn't know Martin had fired her, and he was interested in seeing her. The question then was who had gotten her fired and what should she do about it?

"Whoa, Ms. Rodgers, who did you get the flowers from?" Rhea, one of her students asked as she entered.

One thing was for sure. Gwen would have to take the flowers home. "Just a friend saying thank you."

"That's some thank you." Rhea's statements were echoed by the other students when they entered, and it took an extra ten minutes to get the class on task.

When the clock read three thirty, Gwen packed up her things and picked up the flowers. They were so large they blocked her vision, and she was forced to turn sideways to see where she was going.

"Whoa, that is an armful. Need some help?"

Gwen's heart dropped when she recognized the voice of Tom Boyer, the PE teacher. He had asked her out several times, but Gwen had always turned him down. Not only was he not her type, but he cursed like a sailor. Gwen couldn't stand the sound of curse words, never used them, and had made a promise she would never be with anyone who did. Unfortunately, Tom hadn't taken her declining his offer well. He'd made it a point to stop by her classroom at least once a week, always with the ruse that he was discussing a student but really, he simply wanted to compliment her.

"No, I'm fine, thank you." She kept her tone friendly, hoping he would get the hint and leave her alone. No such luck.

"Someone die?" He said it like a joke, but Gwen didn't find it funny. She hadn't wanted flowers when her parents were killed. She had simply wanted them back. He had probably never lost anyone close to him if he could joke about death so callously.

"No, they're from a guy I'm seeing." Gwen didn't mean to lie. The words slipped out before she could rein them in, however, they did have the intended effect. A look of disbelief crossed Tom's features followed by one of resignation, but he did drop the pursuit and walk away. Unfortunately, Gwen also knew he wouldn't keep the knowledge to himself. By tomorrow, everyone would want to know about this new mystery man.

With a sigh, she continued to her car but paused when she reached it. Her eyes flicked from the front seat to the flowers. It would be a tight squeeze just to fit them in. She slung her purse in the backseat first and then maneuvered the flowers into the passenger seat. They filled most of the seat, and she debated buckling them in with the seatbelt but decided against it. She looked comical enough as it was.

The drive back to her house was slow though. Every time she tapped the brakes, she feared the flowers would tumble off the seat and onto the floor, and her arm would shoot across as if protecting a child.

When she reached her apartment, she circled it once to see if any of her nosy neighbors were out. An elderly woman lived a few doors down and made it her mission to know everything that was going on in the apartment. While Gwen didn't normally mind the woman or her curiosity, she had no desire to answer the woman's questions tonight. Thankfully, the woman was nowhere to be seen.

As quickly as she could, Gwen parked the car, grabbed the flowers and her personal items, and hightailed it into her apartment. Only when the door shut behind her, did she allow her guard to drop.

Gwen placed the flowers on her small bar and pulled out her cell phone. She needed Carrie and her advice.

Half an hour later, Carrie arrived at the front door, bags of Chinese food in her hands.

"I've got fo…. whoa, are those from Drew Devonshire?" she asked as she stepped into the room.

"Who else would they be from? That arrangement had to cost a few hundred dollars."

Carrie set the bags on the table and walked closer to the flowers. A low whistle escaped her lips. "At least. Please tell me you'll see him again now."

Gwen sucked in her breath. She still wasn't sure. After her last class had left, she had decided to call - she needed to at least find out if he knew about her being fired - and then chickened out. The first time, she had barely touched the phone. The second time, she managed to dial the first number. The last time, she managed to dial all but the last number. But she just couldn't complete the call.

"He didn't have to send flowers, you know," Carrie said. "He had already given back the bracelet. He had no reason to connect with you again."

"Unless it was to apologize for getting me fired. If that's the case, flowers aren't enough."

"Was there a card?"

Gwen sighed. "There was, but he didn't mention an apology. Could he really not know though?"

Carrie folded her arms across her chest and cocked her head. "Well, there's one way to find out."

"I know, but what do I even say to him?"

"I don't know," Carrie said, punctuating her words with an eye roll. "How about thank you for starters?"

Gwen stared down at her cell phone. Could she do it? Could she call him?

"Come on. I'll be right here for moral support."

Her fingers trembled as she punched in the numbers. Then the sound of a ring reached her ears.

*D*rew read over the paperwork again. Fate had dealt Gwen Rodgers a rough hand. Her parents had died in an auto accident shortly after her twelfth birthday. Drew couldn't even imagine. How did you go to bed one night and wake up the next day with no family? Not surprisingly, the police report stated that Gwen had been almost unresponsive when given the news.

Then, she had been taken into Child Protective

Service custody. Drew knew that most of the time, the case workers did great work and found wonderful homes for children who needed a safe place, but he also knew bad people slipped through the cracks. It appeared Gwen's first house had been one of the latter. The father had apparently locked her in a closet and fed her through a small door. She had been deprived of sunlight for nearly a week until the school had finally called the case worker looking for her. Why it had taken a week was beyond Drew, and he could only imagine how traumatized Gwen must have been. In fact, considering all she had been through, it was amazing she was as well-adjusted as she seemed now. What had made that difference?

Beside him the phone rang, and he picked it up without bothering to check the caller ID. Few people had his personal number, so it was probably his mother anyway. "This is Drew."

There was a pause, and then a quiet voice said, "Hi, Drew, this is Gwen Rodgers."

Instantly, he gripped the phone tighter and turned all his attention to the call. "Hello, Gwen. Did you receive the flowers?" He wanted to smack himself as the words left his mouth. Of course, she had gotten the flowers. Otherwise, she wouldn't have his number.

"I did, and um thank you, but I need to ask what they were for."

For? He thought back to what he had written on the note. Hadn't he said what they were for? "They were a thank you for the lovely evening of the masquerade ball and an offering in hopes you would let me take you out."

"So, they weren't an apology?"

Drew's brow knitted together. An apology? Was there something he needed to apologize for? "I'm not sure I know what you mean."

There was a small sigh on the other end. "I was fired last night from my catering job."

"What? Gwen, I didn't do that. I would never have asked them to fire you."

"I believe you," she said, "but someone did. Do you know who might have done that?"

Drew had an idea. His mother had been upset at the scene. If anyone had said anything to her, she might have retaliated. "Gwen, I'm so sorry. It might have been my mother. This is all my fault."

"No, it's my fault. I should never have been at the ball."

"Gwen, let me make it up to you. What do you need?" He didn't think she would take his money, but he was offering it anyway. "Do you want me to speak to your boss?"

Gwen scoffed on the other end. "Don't bother. It won't do any good. I'll find another job somewhere."

He could help with that. From looking over her paperwork, he knew she donated a little money to a foster care charity. "What if I could give you a job?"

Gwen's answer was a nervous chuckle. "I wasn't looking for a pity hire, Drew."

Man, she was perceptive, but maybe he could play it off. "It's not a pity hire. I've been looking for new tax write offs, and I know we don't donate all we are allowed. It wouldn't be a lot of hours, but I could use someone who has a passion for a cause to handle our donations."

There was a pause on the other end. "How do you know I have a passion for a cause?" Her voice was hesitant.

Drew bit the inside of his lip. He wasn't ready to tell her he had been looking into her. "I'm sorry, I just figured since your church seemed so important to you that you might support a cause. Don't church people do that?" he finished lamely.

"Have you ever been to church?" Gwen's voice held a note of disbelief.

"A few times, but I'm certainly not a regular attender. I'm sorry if I assumed incorrectly. If you don't want the job, I'm sure I can find someone else-" As he hoped it would, the reverse psychology spurred Gwen into action.

"No, don't do that. I'd be delighted to take that on for you. I have a few charities very dear to my heart, and I would love the opportunity to send more money their way."

"Wonderful. Can you meet me at the Kingston tomorrow?" The Kingston was another of their hotels. Drew didn't want to meet at the Devonshire for fear of running into his mother, but she rarely visited the Kingston leaving the management of it up to him.

"I work until four, but I could meet you there after?" The hesitation was back in Gwen's voice and made her statement come off like a question. Was it due to his meeting choice?

"How about five? I'll meet you in the lobby, we can discuss business, and then perhaps we can partake of some food." He, on the other hand, phrased his request as a declaration. He had learned long ago that confidence won a lot of battles.

"I can do five. Do I need to bring anything?"

"Your ID and Social. I'm sure it won't be an issue, but we run a background check on all our employees." This was perfect. Hiring her had been a spur-of-the-moment decision, but now he wouldn't have to act like he didn't know about her past.

"Understood. I'll see you then."

As Drew hung up the phone, he couldn't help but feel a little excitement at the prospect of seeing Gwen again. Even better, he was going to have her near him at least once a week. The way he saw it, this was a win-win situation all around.

CHAPTER 8

"You feel like getting a coffee?"

Drew looked up from the reports he was studying to see Avery, looking pressed and pristine in the doorway of his office.

"Sure. I need a break from these anyway. Quarterly reports always mire down my day."

"Grab your coat then. There's a place just down the block I've really missed."

Drew nodded, wondering if the place she was referring to was Chez Cafe. It was a trendy, hipster place just around the corner that served specialty coffee and French pastries, and it was one of his favorite places as well.

He shrugged into his Burberry coat and plucked the scarf from the coat rack. The air had turned quite chilly today, almost as if the weather knew it was now November and therefore it needed to plunge into freezing temperatures to prepare for the first snowfall.

"Won't you need a coat?" he asked as his eyes roamed her frame. Her pantsuit was designer and expensive, but it didn't appear very warm.

"I left it with your doorman," she said with a flick of her hand. "It's too warm in here to wear it. Plus, it makes me look twenty pounds heavier. Perhaps I should design a coat that still shows off a woman's curves."

"You could do that," Drew said biting back a smile. Avery was not one who accepted defeat, and he knew if he told her she wasn't a designer that she would do all she could to prove him wrong.

"No, I couldn't." She rolled her eyes at him. "I'm an artist, not a designer."

"Well, I'm sure you could hire someone who could design it for you." Fitted coats was not a topic of conversation Drew wanted to continue further. He didn't care about a woman's coat. In truth, he rarely noticed them. Eyes were what he focused on. There was so much you could see in someone's eyes, especially someone of depth. Like Gwen's eyes who had haunted his visions since the night of the ball.

"Now that is not a bad idea." With a purposeful stride, Avery led the way into the foyer. Her heels clacked against the marble flooring, and Drew couldn't help but notice the subtle swaying of her hips. Was that for him or had she always walked that way? He couldn't remember, but it had been years since he had seen her. She could have acquired the trait along the way.

She paused just long enough to rescue her coat from the

doorman and then she was stepping out into the dreary grey weather. The wind pulled at Drew's coat with icy fingertips as he followed her as if trying to peel away his warmth. Drew loved winter - the snow, the colors, the general feeling of good will, but he wasn't a fan of the biting cold. Not unless he could be home in front of his fireplace with a warm cup of coffee and a good movie.

"So, are you back for good?" he asked quickening his stride to pull even with her.

"For the foreseeable future. I ran out of money in Europe, starving artist and all that. Father wouldn't extend me any more credit. So, now I'm back until I can earn enough money to continue doing what I love."

Drew understood that feeling. It was similar to his situation, and he wasn't sure he'd ever get out of the hotel business now.

Avery pulled open the door to Chez Cafe, and a friendly wave of warmth rolled out to greet them. A low hum of conversation buzzed around the crowded room. "It might be standing room only in here."

"A table will open up," Avery said with a wave of her hand. "It always does."

The line moved quickly and within minutes they were at the front placing their order. "I'll have an Iced, Half Caff, Ristretto, Venti, 4-Pump, Sugar Free, Cinnamon, Dolce Soy Skinny Latte," Avery said.

Drew blinked at her. Her words might have been English, but he had no idea what she had even ordered. Surprisingly though, the barista behind the register just nodded and scribbled something on a cup. As Drew never understood the markings on the cup either, he wondered if the employees had some kind of code for snobby drink orders.

"And for you?" the woman asked as Avery stepped to the side.

"Just an Americano with room for cream please."

The woman raised an eyebrow at him but said nothing. However, a small smile played across her lips.

"See? I told you a table would open up." Avery pointed to a small round table shoved in the far corner. "I'm going to go claim it. You get the drinks, okay?"

Before he could answer, she had walked off. Drew bit the inside of his lip and nodded ever so slightly. Now, he was beginning to remember why they had broken up. Avery might not be as obsessed with status as some other women, but she was independent and just a little bossy.

"Here's your friend's drink," the woman said. "Your Americano will be right up."

"Thank you." Drew took Avery's drink and surreptitiously scanned the barista's writing. A series of letters that looked more like hieroglyphics than English stared back at him. Before he could ponder it further, the woman handed him his drink, and Drew meandered through the tables to Avery.

"So," she said when he sat down, "what happened with the girl from last night?"

"What do you mean?" he asked.

"I was there remember?" She took a sip of her drink.

"You made quite the scene, and you were telling me about this woman you met at your mother's ball. Was she the one?"

Drew lifted his own cup and pretended to drink. He wasn't sure how much he should tell Avery. He didn't think she would go running to his mother, but it had been years since they were close. Perhaps she had changed in that time. He opted for a diversion. "Did you know we got that poor woman fired?"

Avery blinked at him. "We did?"

"Well, someone did. I presume it was my mother, but I suppose it could have been anyone in the room."

"And how do you know she was fired?" Avery tilted her head as she regarded him.

Dang it. He was off his game today. Perhaps he could get away with a half-truth. "I spoke with her, and she informed me."

Avery nodded slowly. "Just out of the blue you spoke with this woman? This woman who wasn't supposed to be at your mother's ball and works as a caterer?"

It was clear Avery would not let this go. With a sigh, Drew filled her in. "All right, I sent her flowers and asked her to call me."

"You proposed a date?" Avery let out a soft whistle. "I don't know your mother well, but I can't imagine she would want you pursuing a caterer."

"She's a full-time teacher." Drew felt the need to point out Gwen's qualities though he wasn't sure why. Avery wouldn't care who he pursued. "She was catering on the side to earn extra money. At least until she got fired."

"Well, that's," Avery paused as if searching for the right word, "noble. Teaching, I mean. The world needs good teachers, right?"

Avery's words sounded stilted and forced. Drew wondered what she had against teachers. Or was this a snobby bias of hers emerging?

"Yes, we need good teachers, and I'm sure she is one."

Avery sighed. "Drew, what do you even know about this woman?"

He wanted to tell her he knew a lot, but something gave him pause. Avery didn't need to know he had dug into Gwen's background. "I know she isn't obsessed with money and status like everyone else around us. She's funny and genuine, and she made me feel alive again."

Avery's stare burned into him. "I get that you don't want to pursue someone in the elite circle, but I hope you know what you're doing, Drew."

*G*wen glanced at the clock. It was four already? She was surprised that the time had seemed to fly by and even more surprised that no one had hounded her asking for details on the new boyfriend. Had Tom not said anything then? That seemed unlike him, but maybe he had kept it to himself out of pride. Most of the staff knew of his interest in her. Admitting she was seeing someone else would be like accepting his defeat, and Gwen doubted he had done that.

With a sigh, she stacked the remaining papers to grade in front of her laptop. She had learned long ago not to take work home because she never graded it. The papers merely received a field trip - into her bag, into her car, sometimes even into her house, but inevitably they never left her bag again until she brought them back to school the next day. No, these could wait for tomorrow. She would just have to focus during her planning time to get them graded.

Gwen grabbed her coat and keys and made her way to the parking lot. Menacing grey clouds filled the sky, and she wondered if the first snow might come early this year. The temperature certainly had dropped enough. She'd even had to scrape ice off her window this morning, something she didn't usually have to do until after Thanksgiving.

Unlocking the car, she slid in and inserted the key. She was anxious to get the heater on. The heated seats of her car were the one upgrade she had purchased when she bought the used vehicle. Carrie had them in her Range Rover, and Gwen had fallen in love with them. There was something comforting about the warmth against her back and legs.

As they heat seeped through her layers, Gwen pointed the car toward her house. She would have just enough time to duck inside and change into something a little nicer before meeting Drew. She didn't know if she needed to dress up, but it felt enough like a job interview that she wasn't comfortable going in her slacks and cotton shirt.

After a quick stop to change and freshen up, Gwen

pulled into the parking lot of the Kingston. She had never been inside this hotel though she thought it was older than the Devonshire. Not that it mattered; Gwen had neither the money nor the reason to stay at a hotel.

An older gentleman with graying hair but kind eyes opened the door as she approached. "Welcome to the Kingston, Miss," he said with just a hint of a British accent.

"Thank you. Do you know where I can find Mr. Devonshire?" Gwen was sure he had an office somewhere, but she didn't want to wander the hotel looking for it.

"Are you Miss Rodgers?"

Gwen blinked at the man. His knowledge of her name caught her off guard. "I am."

The man's lips pulled into a soft smile. He looked like what Gwen had always imagined a grandfather would look like. She barely remembered her own. Her mother's mother had died when she was four and her mother's father when she was ten. She had never met her father's parents as they had passed on before she was born.

"I am to take you to his office if that's agreeable with you." He offered his arm, clad in a blue jacket. White gloves covered his hands.

Gwen hesitated only a moment. Was she becoming more trusting or did he just not radiate a dangerous vibe? With her hand on his arm, he led the way to the back of the hotel. "Your guest, Mr. Devonshire," the doorman said as they entered Drew's office.

Drew looked up and smiled. "Ah, thank you, Fletcher. Come on in, Gwen."

Fletcher patted her hand once before turning and walking back down the hallway. Gwen stepped farther into the room and stood awkwardly behind one of the chairs. Should she sit? Was there paperwork?

"Sit, sit," he said as if reading her mind. "I am required to have you fill out some paperwork for legal, and then I'll show you where you can work."

Gwen walked to the front of the chair and sat down. Her heart hammered in her chest, and she wasn't sure if she was nervous about the job or about being near Drew again. Probably, it was a combination of both.

"Let's see." He shuffled through the papers on his desk. His mind must work in a similar way to hers because he looked a little like organized chaos as well. The corners of her lips pulled up as she watched him.

"Ah, here we go." He pulled out a few sheets and slid them across the large desk to her. "Basic application plus a background check. Did you bring your ID?"

It was weird being in the room with him like this. She still felt an attraction to him, but his tone was all business. However, the flowers had suggested he wanted more. Her stomach knotted in confusion and she dropped her face to cover the pink she knew covered it. "Yeah, sure, just a second."

She pulled her wallet out and slipped the ID from its holder. Gwen grimaced at the picture as she handed it across to him. She never took pictures well and IDs were the worst, but she looked like a deer in the headlights in this picture.

Her eyes were too wide, and instead of a smile, her lips had formed a slight "oh" shape.

He took the ID from her and perused it. Flames of embarrassment licked up her neck. "Doesn't look much like you," he said. His eyes twinkled, and she knew he was teasing, but it didn't ease her self-consciousness. "But I guess not many people take good ID photos," he continued as if sensing her unease. "Let me go make a copy and I'll return shortly."

Gwen nodded and turned her attention back to the form. It appeared to be a standard application. Name, address, social, job history. She put the pen to the paper and began the tedious task.

"Drew, I forgot to ask you…." A female voice filled the room behind Gwen, and she turned her head to see the woman from the other night behind her. She had assumed when she first glimpsed the woman at the table with Drew that she was a girlfriend, but then he had asked her out when he followed her into the hallway. However, the woman appearing now in Drew's office suggested she knew him well.

"Oh, I'm sorry," the woman said as her eyes roamed over Gwen. "I was looking for Drew. Do you know when he might be back?"

Gwen opened her mouth to answer, but never got the chance.

"He's back now," Drew said, appearing behind the woman. "What can I do for you, Avery?"

Gwen was pleased to hear confusion in his voice. It appeared he had not planned for the woman's arrival.

Avery smiled, revealing perfectly white teeth. "Well, I was going to ask you if you found a solution to the little problem you were telling me about earlier, but perhaps this is it?" She finished the statement like a question, her voice lilting up just slightly at the end, and her raised eyebrow and glance at Gwen emphasizing it.

Drew pushed past her, his face tight as if clenching his jaw. "Avery, I'd like you to meet Gwen Rodgers. I've just hired her to manage donations for the Devonshire hotel." His voice carried a pinched quality, and Gwen wondered why he didn't seem to want Avery to know about his hiring her. Was he ashamed of her? Were they together?

Avery glided across the room like a graceful ballerina. "Gwen, it is so nice to meet you. Any friend of Drew's is a friend of mine." On the outside, her words were friendly as was her gesture to shake hands, but Gwen somehow doubted they would ever be friends.

"Thanks for stopping by, Avery," Drew said, "but I need to finish up with Gwen here and give her the information to get started."

Avery blinked, a sign that she wasn't used to Drew addressing her in such a manner, but she said nothing about it. Instead, her lips stretched into an even wider grin. "Of course, I'll leave you two alone. I'm sure I'll be seeing a lot more of you, Gwen." She held Gwen's gaze a moment, but Gwen wasn't entirely certain if her words were a promise or a threat.

"My apologies," Drew said when Avery had left the room. "I had no idea she would show up here."

"Oh, it's fine. I mean your girlfriend is none of my business."

Drew's brow arched. "Girlfriend? No, no. Avery and I dated once years ago, but we're too alike in too many areas to make it work."

"Oh." Gwen hated the thrill of excitement that raced through her at those words. It didn't matter if Avery wasn't his girlfriend. She wasn't either, and while he and Avery might be too similar, she and Drew were too different to make it work.

"Besides, I thought I made it clear with those flowers that I was interested in pursuing you."

There was no way to stop the heat that consumed her face this time. His gaze was frank and honest as his eyes sought hers.

"Drew, I already told you-"

"And I think you're wrong," he said interrupting her. "Look, just let me take you to dinner. If it doesn't work out, at least we can say we tried."

Gwen ran through her options. She wanted to see him again. He was asking. It was just dinner. "All right. Dinner, but only if I can pick the place."

"Fine, you pick the place. How about tomorrow night?"

Gwen bit her lip but nodded. "Tomorrow night is fine. Let's meet at Charlie's at seven. Are you familiar with it?"

His brow furrowed as if he was exerting energy running down a mental list. "I'm not, but I'm sure my driver is."

Of course, he wasn't familiar with it. Charlie's was a dive, but it served great food. Gwen wondered what his reaction would be. "That will work then."

Drew returned the smile. "Good. Now that that's taken care of, shall I show you your workspace?"

"Lead the way."

CHAPTER 9

*D*rew stared into his closet the next night. He hadn't dressed casually since college, but his search of this restaurant informed him casual would blend in better. The problem was business suits dominated his wardrobe now. Had the trends changed since college? If he wore jeans and a polo would he blend in or stand out?

"Is there a problem, sir?" Pierre asked from behind him.

"I'm not sure how to dress for this date," Drew said. "I'm meeting a woman who is not wealthy, at a bar downtown, and the website said to dress casual."

Pierre's eyebrow rose only slightly. He had been trained not to react, no matter what he saw or heard. "I see. Well, I believe this blue shirt is still very much in style," - he grabbed it off the rack - "and, though I never wear them myself, I have heard Manuel say jeans never go out of style." Pierre handed the jeans and shirt to Drew who nodded and slipped them on.

"You still look very debonair if I may say so, sir."

Drew thought he would feel more uncomfortable but slipping into the jeans felt like rekindling an old friendship. One he hadn't had since college. "Thank you, Pierre. It's different but not altogether bad."

Pierre nodded, and Drew grabbed his wallet and slipped it in his back pocket. With a final glance in the mirror, Drew headed downstairs. Manuel was waiting outside the front door with the limo.

"I almost didn't recognize you, sir," Manuel said as he straightened when Drew approached.

Drew chuckled as he responded, "Good. Maybe no one else will either." He slid into the backseat surprised to feel his heart beating faster than normal. Was that because he would see Gwen or because he was a little nervous about walking into an unfamiliar restaurant? "You know what, Manuel? Can you drop me off at the end of the block?"

"Sir?" Drew always preferred being dropped off at the door, but this time, he didn't want to show off his money. He wanted to pretend to be a little normal.

"This isn't my usual venue, Manuel. I'd prefer not to draw so much attention."

"Understood, sir."

Half an hour later, the car slowed to a stop. Drew glanced out the window. The restaurant appeared to be half a block ahead on the right if the garish neon light was any indication.

"Here we are, sir."

"Thank you, Manuel. I'll get the door." Drew knew it

probably made Manuel uncomfortable, but he stayed in the driver's seat and allowed Drew to open the back door himself. "I'll text when I'm ready," Drew said before shutting the door. He waited for the limo to drive off, then smoothed his shirt, took a deep breath, and continued up the sidewalk to the eating establishment.

Gwen sat at a booth in the corner where she could see the entrance. She had arrived ten minutes early hoping to see Drew when he entered. She wanted to gauge his reaction. This was one of her favorite places to grab a burger and if he couldn't fit in, she would take it as a sign this was not meant to be.

Her eyes flew to the entrance every time the door opened, but she still almost missed Drew when he entered. Gone was the Armani suit. Instead, he wore a blue button-down shirt and jeans. He still held the air of someone with money, but he didn't stand out from the rest of the clientele. She raised her hand as his eyes scanned the room. When he noticed her hand, he smiled and started her direction.

"You found it," she said as he slid in across from her.

"I did, or my driver did."

"Does he drive you everywhere?" Gwen couldn't imagine not driving herself places. On one hand, it would be nice to curl up with a book while getting to the destination but letting someone else drive meant having to trust them. There just weren't many people she trusted that much, especially after a drunk driver killed her parents.

"He does. At least since I returned from college." He rolled his eyes. "My mother's stipulation. If you have money, you need to use the advantages it offers."

"So, you drove yourself in college?"

"Yes, I had to have a friend teach me. My parents never allowed me to get my license. They said I would never use it, but when I went to college, I wanted to live like everyone else, and that meant driving myself. Thankfully, I met someone who didn't mind teaching me. I bought an old car and managed to only hit a few things."

His lips pulled into a smile, and something tugged on Gwen's heart. He had a gorgeous smile with perfectly white teeth - not that she expected any less - but it was the dimple in his left cheek that she most enjoyed. Somehow it softened his chiseled features and made him even more handsome.

"To be honest, I miss driving sometimes," he continued. "I mean I get work done in the back, but it's nice to feel the wheel beneath your hands and the pedal under your foot at times."

"I'm not sure I could let someone drive for me." Gwen opened her mouth to say more, but then clamped it shut. She didn't know him well enough or trust him enough to tell him about her parents. Not yet anyway.

"It takes some getting used to." He paused as he glanced around the room. "So, this place is nice."

"I'm sure it's not your normal fare," Gwen said with a smile, "but they have amazing burgers here."

"I do enjoy a good burger."

The waitress appeared then with two glasses of water and a plastic-coated menu. Drew's face scrunched slightly as he took the menu. Gwen wondered when he had last held one of these menus. College probably. The restaurants he attended now more than likely had a single sheet of typed menu offerings. Two or three starters, a few main course options, and dessert. Nothing like this three-page menu filled with pictures and corny names. Drew appeared almost overwhelmed as he scanned all the choices, and then he chuckled.

"What's so funny?" Gwen asked.

"This menu just reminded me of college. Some friends and I used to study late in a fast-food restaurant and one night some guy came in and ordered fries. He proceeded to eat almost all of them and then told the manager they were cold, and he needed another. The manager was a softie and he filled the guy's fries again. The guy sat down, ate almost all of them, and then back to the counter he went. This went on another two times before the manager had it and kicked the guy out. A few days later, there was a story in the newspaper about this guy. Evidently, he had been trying the same scam at every Whataburger in the city and when they realized it, they banned him from all of them."

Gwen smiled and shook her head. "I'll never understand some people. Why take advantage of someone's good nature?"

Before Drew could respond, the waitress appeared. "Welcome to Charlie's. The special today is the Blazin'

Burger and our soup is a chicken tortilla. Would you care for anything else to drink?"

"Do you have any Chardonnay?" Drew asked. He was flipping the pages back and forth. Probably searching for the drink options.

The woman's face creased in confusion. "Uh, no, we don't serve wine, but we have beers on tap."

"Right." Drew's words were slow, unsure. "Um, I'll just have iced tea then. You have that right?"

"Yeah, tea we have. And for you?" The waitress turned her attention to Gwen.

"I'll take a tea as well."

"You got it; I'll give you a few minutes to look over the menu and be right back with those."

Gwen smiled up at the waitress. "Thank you." She glanced over at Drew. "Does anything look good?"

"I have no idea. Do you have a recommendation?"

"The Blazin' Burger is actually my favorite. It has sriracha sauce and an onion ring. Just the right combination of spicy and sweet."

He cocked his head at her. "Can I tell you how refreshing it is to eat with a woman who eats?"

"I'll never be one of those tiny women if that's what you're looking for." Gwen wanted to take back the words as soon as she said them. It was quite presumptive of her to expect he'd want to date her.

He fixed her with an intense stare. "I'm not looking for those kinds of women. I told you I found you refreshing and I meant it."

Gwen's face flamed. She had no idea what he saw in her, but she was flattered.

"Sorry, just a second," he said as his phone chimed in his pocket. He swiped the screen, rolled his eyes slightly, and placed the phone back in his pocket.

"Everything okay?" Gwen asked.

"Yes, just a friend."

Gwen wondered if the friend was Avery but asking didn't seem to be appropriate. After all, this was technically their first date and she had just met Avery yesterday.

"You two have a chance to look over the menu?" the waitress asked as she returned with their iced teas.

Gwen looked to Drew who nodded. "I'll have the Blazin' Burger with onion rings," Gwen said.

The waitress nodded and scribbled it down before looking to Drew. "Make that two," he said as he handed back the menu.

As the waitress walked away, a long pause fell on the conversation. Then, Drew cleared his throat. "I uh hope you don't mind, but I did some research on you in addition to the background check."

"Research?" Gwen blinked at him, unsure what he meant.

"Yes," he took a sip of his tea before continuing, "in my life, it's important to know who people are before you hang around them. I'm sure you understand that some people don't have the best intentions."

While she could understand that, her heart sped up at the thought of him digging into her past. Did he know about her parents? Her foster father? All her sordid secrets? "I'm sure you found that I wasn't after your money."

"I did, but um, I had a question for you."

She twirled her glass on the table as she thought about whether she wanted to hear his question. If it had to do with her past, chances were she didn't want to hear it. However, if they were going to try dating, then she would have to let him in sometime. Finally, she lifted her eyes back to him, granting him silent permission to ask his question.

"There's a lot of hurt in your past," he began, and Gwen bit her lip. She hoped he wouldn't ask for details as she didn't want to ruin the dinner with her troubled past. "But, you seem to be well-adjusted and content. Can I ask how?"

It was a fair question and one that had been asked of her many times in the past, but she didn't know how he would respond to her answer. She took a deep breath as she formulated her response. "God," she said simply.

He blinked at her. "I'm sorry, what?"

She smiled softly. God was the one part of her story she never minded sharing. "God. My parents had been Christians before they died, but I was only twelve. I hit that rebellious teenage streak and was certain I didn't need God. Every Sunday was a fight to get me to go to church, but they never let me *not* go. When they died, God had new meaning to me. He became my replacement father and gave me the strength to not only deal with my parents' death but also everything that came after."

Drew leaned back and regarded her for a moment, and Gwen wondered what he was thinking. Had she scared him away with her talk of God? It wouldn't be the first time, but she was a firm believer that anyone who wouldn't at least listen to her story was no one she wanted to spend more time dating.

"I've never placed much stock in faith," Drew said finally. "My parents were holiday Christians at best - Christmas and Easter when they deemed it important enough to attend - but I've never met anyone like you. To go through such tragedy and emerge with such strength, well I envy you, and so I'd like to inquire. Would you allow me to attend church with you this Sunday?"

This time Gwen blinked. She hadn't been expecting that. For him to have to go or to decide he no longer wanted to see her - *that* she had been expecting, but attend church with her? It was like a dream come true. "Of course, you can."

The waitress returned then with the food, and the conversation stalled while they ate. Gwen couldn't believe how normal eating with him felt. No one had even seemed to notice him. Did he not get hounded by photographers and the press? Or did that only happen to movie stars?

"I'd like to do this again."

She dragged her focus back to him. "Dinner?"

"Yes, dinner, dessert, dancing, you name it. I want to spend more time with you. Would you be amenable to that?" Drew pulled a hundred-dollar bill out of his wallet and placed it in the black folder. Gwen hadn't even noticed the waitress drop it off.

Amenable. She enjoyed the way the way he spoke. On some people, it would come across like putting on airs, but

Drew's use was so effortless that it must have been part of his upbringing. "Yes, I believe I would be amenable to that," she responded with a smile.

"Good." He stood and held out his hand to her. "What are you doing Saturday?"

Gwen took his hand, enjoying the feel of his skin against hers. He led the way through the crowded restaurant to the door and pushed it open.

"As in a few days from now Saturday?" Gwen asked as they stepped outside.

The dimple re-appeared as a smile stole across his features. "That is the one to which I was referring."

"I don't think I have any plans."

"Wonderful." He dropped her hand for a moment to pull out his cell phone. After tapping out a brief message, he replaced the phone in his pocket and took her hand once again. "I know you have an aversion to being driven, but I promise Manuel is a cautious and distinguished driver. I would like to surprise you, so may we pick you up ten am Saturday morning?"

Gwen hesitated. Could she give control to someone else? Someone she didn't know? The thought terrified her; however, she would have to do it someday. Now might be a good time to start.

"All right. I guess I must let go sometime. I'll text you my address."

Drew grabbed her other hand and held them both against his chest. "I promise it will be worth it. I had a great time tonight."

Gwen's heart thudded loudly. "Me too." Though only two words, it took great effort to get them out of her mouth. Her lungs felt tight as if they couldn't get enough air. Their gazes held a moment longer and then a black limo pulled up in front of the parking lot.

A sigh billowed out of Drew's lips. "I see my transportation has arrived. Please drive safely." He brought her hand to his lips, and Gwen watched as he placed a kiss on the back of her hand. His lips were soft, almost like the wings of a butterfly brushing her skin. Tiny goosebumps erupted on her arm. Then Drew winked at her and dropped her hand. "I will see you on Saturday."

Gwen nodded and walked to her car. Her whole body tingled. Why did he have such an effect on her?

CHAPTER 10

*G*wen yawned and stretched as the light peeked in her window. Tiny particles floated in the ray of light creating a shimmery feel in the air. Her lips twitched into a smile as Gwen experienced a similar feeling throughout her body. The events of the week left her with warm and fuzzy thoughts. Though Drew had been too busy to meet up with her, he had called her every night. She hadn't thought she and Drew would have anything in common, but he was much more down-to-earth than she had expected.

She ought to know better. Gwen hated it when people made assumptions about her, especially when they found out about her foster care background. It was odd how quickly people's views shifted with that tidbit of knowledge. Those who couldn't hide their response would do one of two things: they would apologize to her as if the experience had to have been awful or they would look for some excuse to get away from her as if she was contagious. The people who tried to hide their reaction were often worse. They would tense up and shower her with pitying looks and head shakes.

Gwen knew most people didn't even have any first-hand knowledge of the foster care system - they only had what they heard on the news or TV shows which rarely put the system in a good light. Gwen, however, had lived through it, both the good and the bad. And while she wouldn't wish foster care on anyone - a loving biological family was what God intended - it had been there for her at a time when she needed it most. She hoped she could change the perception around foster care which was partly why she accepted Drew's job proposal. The fact that she needed extra income and wanted an excuse to be near him also played a part.

A tremor of excitement raced through her, and she kicked off the comforter. He was picking her up at ten and swore he had a whole day planned. Gwen never had anyone take her on a surprise date, and she had no idea what to expect.

As if he was reading her mind, her phone buzzed on the nightstand beside her. She unplugged the charging cord and tapped the screen.

Good morning. I trust you slept well. I will be arriving promptly at ten. Please have a robe and dress shoes packed.

A robe and dress shoes? Where exactly was he taking her?

She tossed the phone back on her bed and, shaking her head, walked to the bathroom to shower for the day.

Thirty minutes later, she was clean, dressed, and had her

bag packed. Her stomach rumbled as she walked into the kitchen, a reminder that she hadn't eaten yet.

Gwen grabbed the oatmeal from the pantry and poured it into a pot with some almond milk and sugar free hot chocolate. Finding "The Hungry Girl" cookbook had been the highlight of her summer. Having lost her mother so young, Gwen hadn't grown up learning to cook, so a lot of the traditional cookbooks lost her with their fancy ingredients and steps. Lisa Lillian, on the other hand, used everyday ingredients in a lower fat version. And since her recipes were usually only for one or two people, Gwen didn't have to worry about wasting food or having a ton of leftovers.

With the oatmeal heating on the stove, she turned to the coffee pot. Gwen didn't really like the taste of coffee - in fact, she loved green tea - but there was something comforting about one cup of coffee flavored with her favorite creamer. She loved curling up in her recliner with it as she read her devotional. Not only was it the best time of the morning, but it always made her feel closer to God.

As she placed the filter in, Gwen heard a sound at her front door. She paused, fingers just touching the rim of the recycled brown filter, but she heard nothing more. Had it been a knock? Or perhaps the sound had been at her neighbor's door and not her own.

The closeness was one thing Gwen abhorred about apartment life. The lack of lawn management, the pool, the weight room - all great benefits, but the fact that she heard the neighbors above her as they argued or the squeaky bed frame of the neighbors beside her drove her nuts. When she could afford it, she wanted a small house on a piece of land, so her neighbors wouldn't be too close.

Gwen poured the coffee grinds in, added the water, and flipped the switch to start the coffee percolating. Now, she could check out the noise. It had probably been nothing but living alone had taught Gwen to trust her sense of sound.

She peered out the spyhole first, but no one stood on her doorstep. Had she imagined it then? Gwen flipped the locks on the door and slowly opened it. If someone was out there, she didn't want to fling the door wide too quickly and make herself a target.

The community area between the two apartments was also vacant, but as Gwen looked around, a black flower caught her eye. Nestled against her front door frame, it lay as if propped there, and further inspection showed a white envelope as well. Gwen leaned farther out to scan the area, but whoever had left the note was gone.

Her heart thudded in her chest as she grabbed the envelope and the flower. It was a rose. Painted black. Black roses didn't exist naturally, at least not unless the Turkish black rose was real, but Gwen had her doubts. However, the black rose had two meanings - passion or foreboding death. Drew had already sent her flowers - a large colorful display, so this didn't seem his style which meant the sender probably hadn't been intending passion.

She shut and locked the door. Should she open this? Call the police? Calling the cops might be jumping the gun, but what if someone sent her poison in the envelope? That happened, right? Well, not to people like her. Maybe if she were well known, some celebrity or politician or something, but Gwen was a simple school teacher.

Crossing to the kitchen, Gwen set the rose down on her table and then turned the envelope over. It was completely white, not even her name on it. Maybe it wasn't for her after all. Maybe someone had put it at the wrong door. It was easy to do that in an apartment complex.

The envelope wasn't sealed however, so Gwen lifted the flap and pulled out the note. It was white card stock with typed black lettering. 'Cinderella wasn't real' was all the note said. Not that threatening in and of itself but combined with the black rose, Gwen didn't have warm fuzzies. And though there was no name, the note had to be for her. While Drew wasn't a prince, he certainly represented the wealthy elite and she the poor parentless girl.

The question was…. Who would send this? It could have been Tom. Though he had said nothing the rest of the week, she was sure his ego was still suffering, and he could have easily found out where she lived. But the black rose didn't seem his style. Neither did the simple, elegant card. Tom was much more literal. Saying it to her face or spreading rumors was more like him.

So, Avery? Gwen didn't know her well, but she had been dressed stylishly. Elegant would certainly describe her, and Gwen had sensed some tension from the woman. Perhaps she still harbored feelings for Drew? But how would she know where Gwen lived? Had she returned while Drew had been showing Gwen around and gotten her address off the paperwork? Gwen would have to ask Drew if he thought Avery capable of such a thing.

A bubbling sound reached her ears, and Gwen dropped the envelope. Her oatmeal. She hurried over to the stove and turned the heat off. She was lucky her pot was copper or else she would have a sticky disaster on her hands. Gwen scraped the oatmeal into a bowl and poured her coffee into a mug.

She would come back to the envelope later, but for now it was time to eat and do her devotional. Gwen felt like she needed it more than ever this morning. She needed clarity on what to do with this whole situation. Did she continue seeing Drew? End it now?

*D*rew whistled as he dressed Saturday morning. He couldn't wait to spend the day with Gwen. He had spent much of yesterday planning it. He and Manuel would pick her up at ten. Manuel would drive them to the airport, and they would take the jet to Martha's Vineyard. Once there, he had even more planned: a massage, an afternoon wine and cheese pairing, and dinner at the finest restaurant.

A knock sounded at the door and then Pierre stepped into the room. "I have your wallet, sir. The tickets are there as well."

"Thank you, Pierre." Even when he hated the requirements that came with money, he never hated Pierre. The man helped him stay organized, and most days, he seemed to read Drew's mind and know what he needed before Drew did.

Drew grabbed the wallet off the tray and slid it into the back pocket of his tan Gucci pants. The tickets he inserted into the breast pocket of his jacket before nodding at Pierre and making his way downstairs.

Manuel was waiting out front with the limo, and half an hour later, they were pulling to a stop in an apartment parking lot. Drew stared up at the buildings scrunched so close together. He hadn't been near buildings like these since college. Wanting to experience the college life, he had lived in a dorm for one semester. That had been all he could handle. After that semester, he had rented a large house near campus.

"I'm sorry, sir, this is as close as I can get," Manuel said from the front seat. "Would you like me to park and get the door?"

"No, keep the engine running. I can manage the door." Drew pulled the handle and stepped out of the limo. A man in flannel pajamas carrying a trash bag stopped and stared as Drew scanned the buildings for identification. He must look as out of place as he felt.

Relief filled Drew when he spotted the G on the closest building. Gwen lived in 4G. With purposeful steps, he strode that direction and rapped on her door. It swung open a moment later, and a smile pulled at his lips. Gwen looked simple and radiant in her jeans and hunter green sweater, but there was a pinched look to her face.

"What is the matter?" he asked.

"Can you come inside a minute?"

"Of course. One moment." He tapped out a message to Manuel to let him know they'd be another few minutes and then stepped into her apartment. Though small, it was decorated simply and neatly.

"You know Avery well, right?" Gwen asked as she walked toward the kitchen.

Why would she be asking about Avery? Hadn't he assured her there was nothing going on there? "I do, or at least I did. She left for a few years after we parted ways, but why are you inquiring about Avery?"

"I received something this morning and I want to know if you think she sent it." Gwen picked up an elegant black rose and note and handed them to him.

'Cinderella wasn't real.' He read the typed script and looked up at her. "How did you receive them?"

"Someone left them on my doorstep this morning. Would she do this?"

Drew didn't think so. Avery stated she wasn't interested in him, and she had appeared friendly to Gwen when they had met. "Was there anything else?"

"Just a plain white envelope." She picked it up and held it out to him.

He examined the envelope and turned it over. No distinct markings. "Are you sure it's even for you? There's no name on it."

She cocked her head at him. "Really? You think Cinderella applies to someone else?"

Drew nodded. While it could apply to someone else, it

was more likely directed at Gwen, but he still didn't think it was Avery. His mother, perhaps? But how would she even know about Gwen? Perhaps Avery had mentioned Gwen to his mother or maybe she had seen the paperwork. "I'm sorry. It might have been Avery, or it might have been my mother though I'm not sure why they would do it this way. Telling me would be more their cup of tea. Could it be anyone you know?"

Gwen shrugged. "There's a man at my work who's asked me out several times even though I keep turning him down. He saw me with the flowers you sent the other day, but this seems too abstract for him."

"I don't want this to ruin our day. How about I take it with us and have someone investigate it? I have a friend on the force who could run it for fingerprints." Though the note and the flower bothered him, he was more worried the incident would cause Gwen to run again.

"Maybe this is a sign, Drew-" Gwen began.

He dropped the items to take her hands. "Gwen, this is not a sign. It's someone's sick idea of a joke, but it is not a sign. Please, don't give up on this yet."

Gwen bit her lip and her green eyes shifted back and forth. "All right, Drew, if you think your friend can help, then I'll let you try."

"Good." He squeezed her hands before dropping them. "Did you pack what I asked you to?"

She narrowed her eyes at him and pursed her lips in an adorable pout. "Yes, though I would like to know why I need a robe and a pair of dress shoes. Those don't normally get paired together. You aren't taking me to some weird artsy thing, are you?"

Drew chuckled and shook his head. Gwen was a breath of fresh air. "No, nothing like that. I promise."

"Okay, then, I guess I'm ready." She said the words, but she didn't move. Drew picked up the items with one hand and held out the other to her. After a glance down and a deep breath, she placed her hand in his. "I need to get my bag by the front door."

"Let's go then." He tugged gently to lead her back to the front door, and after she grabbed her bag and shut the door behind her, he led the way to the limo.

He opened the back limo door for her and helped her slide in. Then he opened the front door. Manuel looked over at him in surprise. Drew placed the items on the seat beside him. "Please don't touch these. I need to have them dusted for prints later." Manuel said nothing. He simply nodded. Drew closed the front door and joined Gwen in the back, pulling the door shut behind him. "To the airport please, Manuel."

"The airport? Where are we going, Drew? I have to be back tonight. I have church in the morning, remember?"

The corners of Drew's mouth pulled into a smile. "Don't worry. You'll be back in plenty of time. We're taking a private jet."

"A private jet? Just how wealthy are you?"

Drew smiled, but he didn't want to talk about his money. He wanted to know more about Gwen. "May I ask you something?" he asked instead of answering her question.

"Maybe." Her eyes held his a moment and then fell to her lap.

"I wanted to inquire why you work in the nursery at your church. You seemed excited by it and I was curious to know more."

As he hoped they would, her eyes lit up, and her shoulders relaxed. "I've always loved kids. In fact, I wanted more siblings, but there were complications with my birth, and my mother couldn't have any more after me. We were discussing adoption as a family, but my parents died before the process was complete. So, I guess I've just always had kids on my heart. It's partly why I became a teacher."

"And the other part?" he asked gently. Now that she was opening up, he didn't want her retreating into her shell again.

Her eyes dropped to her lap, and her volume decreased. "I wanted to help kids like myself. Those in foster care. The ones who think no one cares about them."

She paused for a moment and Drew wanted to tell her that people cared, that he cared, but he knew it would sound trite. Though he couldn't explain his connection to her, he expected she would think it was too early or too fast if he mentioned he cared for her.

"Someday, I think I'd like to foster a few kids. I'm sure you know my story." Her gaze shifted up and she fixed him with a penetrating stare.

"A little," he admitted, "but I'd enjoy hearing more about it from you."

She shook her head. "The past is just that. Past. But I

had a not so good family and then a good family. If I can help keep kids from falling in with families like my first, then I want to do it. I can't solve the foster care problem, but I can help. That's what I hope to do with your money. Thank you for the opportunity."

"I'm happy to help. You said people would help if they knew how. I didn't know there was such a need, but now that I do, I'm glad I can do something."

"Well, thank you."

CHAPTER 11

*G*wen studied Drew for a moment. He was not how she pictured billionaires at all. Yes, he rode around in a limo which was unnecessary and wore designer clothing, but he also seemed genuinely interested in helping others. And he appeared interested in her though she had nothing to offer him.

As they pulled into the airport, Gwen tried not to show her awe when the private jet came into view. She had never been on a plane, much less a private jet. "How often do you fly?"

"Not as often as you'd think," Drew said with a small chuckle. "Most of the time, I drive, but occasionally I have to check out a hotel on the other side of the states. I prefer to avoid the airport hassle if you know what I mean." The door opened, and Drew stepped out and then held out his hand to her.

Gwen didn't. She'd heard stories, but she'd never

experienced it firsthand having neither the money nor the reason to fly anywhere. Gwen took his hand and stepped out as well.

A woman in a smart blue skirt and jacket stood at the top of the stairs leading into the plane. "Good morning, Mr. Devonshire," she said as they approached.

"Good morning, Margaret. This is my friend, Gwen."

Margaret turned warm brown eyes on Gwen and smiled. "Good morning, Gwen. Welcome aboard."

Gwen smiled back as she reached the top step, surprised and pleased that the woman didn't seem to care about her social status or lack thereof. She stepped into the plane, and her jaw dropped.

Though she'd never been on one, Gwen had seen pictures and Carrie spoke of how the rows were squished together and the chairs were uncomfortable, but the space before her didn't look like that at all.

Only eight seats existed in this plane. Two rows of two on one side and two rows of two on the other. The seats themselves were wide and luxurious, covered in cream leather and they appeared to recline.

"Take your pick," Drew said behind her. His breath tickled her ear and set her heart stampeding in her chest again. Why did he have such an effect on her? She barely knew him. Was it the money or could there be something real to her feelings?

She chose a seat by the window, wanting to have a view as they took off, and sat down. The seat was as comfortable as it looked, soft and smooth beneath her fingertips, and, after trying all the buttons, Gwen found it did recline.

Drew sat beside her, a small smile twitching at his lips. Did he find her amusing? She must look like a kid in a candy store.

"Would you care for your normal fare?" Margaret asked a moment later.

"I'm not starving," Drew replied. "Perhaps some champagne and strawberries?"

"Yes, sir."

"Champagne?" Gwen asked. "Are we celebrating something?"

"You saying yes to this date." Drew picked up her hand and laced his fingers through hers. "I'm pleased you agreed."

"I am too," Gwen said. Her eyes flew to the window when she felt the plane move. It was just the faintest sensation as the movement was so smooth, but she could see the landscape flying by outside.

"Is this your first time on a plane?" Drew asked.

Gwen nodded. "I've never had anywhere to go nor could I afford it if I did."

"Oh dear, I'm afraid I will spoil you then. Traditional flights aren't as nice."

A soft snort escaped her lips and she pulled her eyes from the window long enough to glance at him. "I figured."

Drew's phone rang, and he slipped it from his pocket. After a glance at the screen, he silenced it and returned it to his pocket.

"Something important?" Gwen asked.

"No, just a friend. I'll call her back later."

She had no right to be jealous, but that didn't stop the small seed from sprouting in her stomach. Was it Avery or some other woman from Drew's past? He was sure to have many, but she would not press the issue. The last thing she wanted to do was come across as insecure though she felt it in every inch of her body.

Margaret returned a moment later with two flutes of champagne and a bowl of red, ripe strawberries. Gwen had never tasted champagne and she wasn't sure if she liked the way it tickled her nose or not. However, the strawberries delighted her. They had long been her favorite fruit and their emergence into the stores was one of her favorite things about summer. The frozen ones just didn't have the same flavor.

They flew in silence for a time until Drew leaned over her and pointed out the window. "There it is. Martha's Vineyard."

Gwen's eyes widened at the beautiful island below them. Lush and green, it was surrounded by crystal blue water on all sides. "It's breathtaking," she whispered.

*D*rew enjoyed watching Gwen's amazement as they stepped off the plane. He grew up spending a few weeks out of every year at Martha's Vineyard, so the novelty wore off a long time ago for him, but Gwen's features danced with excitement.

"Are you hungry or would you like to visit the spa first?"

"Spa?"

"Yes, I hope you don't mind, but I figured you might enjoy some pampering, so I purchased a spa package for you. It includes a massage and a treatment of your choice."

"I wouldn't even know what to choose," Gwen said with a laugh. "I guess today will be a day of firsts for me as I've never had a massage either, but what about you? What are you going to do while I'm getting pampered?"

"I'll be getting my own. You didn't think I'd let you have all the fun, did you?" In fact, Drew enjoyed a weekly massage. He held a lot of tension in his shoulders. At least that's what his masseuse told him.

Gwen smiled up at him. It was a sweet smile and one he could get used to seeing every day. "All right, the spa it is then."

He took her hand and led her to the limo he had waiting. It wasn't that far into town, but he wanted to spoil her today.

"Did you think of everything?" she asked as the driver held the door open for them.

"I tried." Even as he climbed in, Drew went over the mental list of the rest of the day in his mind. It was just past noon and he expected they would spend two hours at the spa. That left them a few hours to sight see and do the wine and cheese pairing before their dinner reservation at six. And, of course, he needed to get her a dress for dinner.

He settled in next to Gwen and watched as she peered out the window. She was like a kid at Christmas. Her eyes sparkled with awe, and her lips seemed fixed in a permanent smile.

Soon the scenery became filled with colorful gingerbread cottages. "They're all so pretty."

Drew had never paid much attention to the houses, but they were indeed a sight. Reds, pinks, blues, and greens. Each one had a small balcony on the second story and a sitting porch. The railings were also painted. Mostly white but some were yellow and orange.

The limo stopped in front of a bright blue cottage with white trim. A white sign that read Le Chateau hung near the sidewalk and swayed in the breeze. Drew stepped out first when the back door opened and then leaned in to help Gwen out. Hand in hand, they made their way to the front door.

Inside, the house was warm and inviting. A soft yellow light illuminated the area. While decorated nicely, Drew hardly noticed the decor. It was no different from many other spas he had been in.

"Welcome to Le Chateau. My name is Margarite. Have you visited us before?" The woman behind the counter had just the hint of a French accent. Probably born in France but here long enough to lose most of the lilt.

"I have," Drew said, "but it's my friends first time."

Margarite grinned. "I love it when we have new guests." She reached under the counter and pulled out a sheet of paper. As she slid it across, Drew could see it was filled with the services offered. "Did you want a package or the à la carte?"

"Actually, I purchased a package already. Drew Devonshire. I believe it was two options."

She clicked a few buttons on the computer next to her and nodded. "Indeed. Welcome, Mr. Devonshire. Please let me know which two options you would like."

Drew scanned the offerings. The massage was a definite. He had been too busy to make his weekly appointment this last week, but his second option would depend on what Gwen picked. He wanted to be sure he was done before she was.

Drew gave her another few minutes to scan the sheet as this was her first time before turning to her and asking, "What looks good?"

"They all look good," she said with a laugh, "but I think in addition to the massage I'll get the manicure and pedicure. I've never had a pedicure, and they always look so nice."

Drew figured a manicure and pedicure would run an additional hour, so for his second choice he chose an acupuncture session.

"Wonderful," Margarite said. She handed them over release forms. "Please fill these out, and I'll take you back."

"What are the release forms for?" Gwen asked as they took a seat.

"Standard procedure," Drew whispered back. "Too many lawsuits today, so they have to cover their back."

"But is it dangerous? I thought a massage was supposed to be relaxing." Worry furrowed her brow and her bottom lip folded under her teeth.

Drew smiled. "It is. I promise you that two hours from now you will feel like a million dollars."

*D*rew had been right. The massage had been wonderful. Gwen wasn't sure how she'd feel letting another person touch her, but the woman they had assigned her had been understanding and waited until Gwen felt comfortable. About halfway through, she had finally relaxed and enjoyed feeling the stress melt out of her muscles.

But the manicure and pedicure had been even better. The woman had rubbed hot stones over her calves and arms, almost like a second massage. And while Gwen had giggled and squirmed a little when the woman scrubbed the bottom of her feet, she had managed to stay still the rest of the time and now sported a lovely reddish orange color on her hands and feet. It was almost the exact shade of her hair. Gwen had loved it so much, she had even written the name down on a business card. She had hoped to buy a bottle, but the twenty-five-dollar price discouraged her. That money could be spent better elsewhere.

"So, how do you feel?" Drew asked as she emerged from the salon room. He must have finished before she did as he rose from a chair in the lobby.

"Like a million dollars," she said with a sly grin. Maybe it was the polish or maybe the relaxation, but she felt freer, less timid.

"You look like a million dollars too," he said. "Ready for the next adventure?"

"There's more?" Gwen asked. Secretly, she was glad. While she had enjoyed the pampering, she found it odd their date was spent mostly apart instead of together.

"Much more." He held out his arm and she placed her hand on the crook. Gwen savored the feeling coursing through her. He treated her like such an elegant lady even holding the door open for her. They turned left away from the limo.

"We're not driving?" she asked.

"The next stop isn't far, and I thought you might enjoy seeing more of the town up close."

Gwen sneaked a glance at him. Was he reading her mind? As they walked, he told her of his summers spent on the island as a boy. She could almost see him running up and down this sidewalk or flying a kite at the nearby beach they had driven past.

Drew stopped in front of a quaint bistro. "Here we are." He held the door open for her and Gwen stepped inside. The room had a large wine bar at the back and several tables for sitting throughout the room. Most were filled with other patrons and a low buzz of conversation filled the air.

"Grab a seat. We'll be right with you," a man hollered from behind the bar.

Gwen followed Drew to a table for two near the window. She was delighted the table had been free, so she could watch the people outside. Studying people had long fascinated her, probably because she'd retreated into her shell for so long. "So, what are we doing here?" she asked. "Is this lunch?" Gwen hadn't noticed it before but now she could feel a slight rumbling in her stomach.

"Well, they don't serve a full lunch here, but I've ordered us a wine and cheese tasting."

"Wine and champagne? Are you trying to ply me with liquor, Drew Devonshire?"

Though she said the words in a teasing tone, his eyes widened, and he shook his head. "No, that wasn't my intention at all. It never even crossed my mind. If you'd rather not drink the wine-"

Gwen smiled and placed a hand on his. "Relax, Drew. First, I was kidding. Second, it's been two hours since the champagne. I think I'm fine." She hadn't had much champagne on the flight anyway. The bubbly sensation had just been too odd.

Drew sighed. "I'm sorry. I planned out this wonderful day for you, and I didn't want you to think I had ulterior motives."

For some reason, Gwen found this side of him even more endearing. People today were so willing to jump into bed with anyone and everyone they met that it was nice to find someone who wasn't looking for that, at least not on the first date. She wasn't sure where intimacy fit on his timeline, and before they got too serious, she would have to let him know that it wasn't on hers until after marriage. But that could wait. Gwen wasn't even sure he would want to see her again though he appeared to be enjoying himself as well.

"I'm glad to hear it, and I didn't think that of you. You've been nothing but a gentleman, and I thank you."

Relief flooded Drew's face, and his posture relaxed.

"Sorry about the wait," the man from behind the bar said as he approached their table. "It's been busy this afternoon. What can I do for you?"

"I ordered a wine and cheese tasting," Drew said as he pulled the tickets from his pocket. "Under the name Devonshire."

The man's eyes widened as if he knew who Drew Devonshire was. He scanned the tickets before handing them back. "Of course, Mr. Devonshire. I'll be right back."

"Do you ever get used to that?" Gwen asked as the man hurried away.

"What?" Drew asked.

"People changing the way they act around you when they find out who you are. It feels so disingenuous."

A deep laugh escaped Drew's lips. "Yes, I guess it is, and that is why you are refreshing, Gwen Rodgers. You didn't change when you knew who I was."

"Well, to be fair, you told me who you were within the first few minutes, so you can't really say I didn't change."

"Touché," Drew said. Laughter danced in his blue eyes. "But I'm not sure you believed me when I first told you who I was."

This time it was Gwen's turn to smile. "I didn't. Truthfully, the only reason I went with you is because I doubted you could abduct me or attack me in such a public place."

The laughter faded from Drew's eyes as her words sank in. He stared at her a moment before speaking. "Gwen, I'm so sorry your past has you thinking things like that about strangers. That's no way to go through life."

Gwen bit her lip to keep her emotions at bay. She couldn't believe she had said that. She hadn't meant to put a damper on the mood. When she trusted her voice not to crack, she opened her mouth to respond. "I wouldn't wish my past on anyone, but it made me have to rely on God and for that I'm thankful."

The server appeared then with their wine and cheese and Gwen was grateful for the distraction. The topic had gotten too heavy for a second date, and she hoped the food would lighten the mood and bring them back to their playful banter from before.

"**W**hat's next?" Gwen asked when their cheese and wine was gone.

Drew stood and held out his hand. "Next, you let me treat you like a princess."

Gwen shook her head as she took his hand and stood. "You already have been treating me like a princess. What more could you possibly do?"

Drew's lips split in a wide smile. "My dear, you have seen nothing yet." Generally, the very thought of taking a woman shopping reduced him to yawns and tears of boredom, but he could tell it would be an adventure with Gwen.

He pushed the door open and led the way to a clothing shop down the street.

"Drew, I don't need any clothes," she said as he pulled open the door.

"I'm not purchasing you a whole wardrobe, Gwen, but you do need a dress for tonight. Remember, robe and dress shoes?"

A soft pink color spread across her cheeks like watercolor on a painting. He adored the look of the blush on her skin. Even more, he enjoyed putting it there. It wasn't often he could get reactions like this from women in his circle. They expected this treatment, and if they ever sported a color on their face, it was generally more often from anger when they didn't get what they wanted.

The shop, while small, housed a myriad of upscale clothing and before they had stepped very far in, a blond woman in a smart tailored suit approached them.

"Welcome, my name is Claire. How may I assist you today?"

"We need a dress. Something simple and elegant for dinner tonight."

The woman nodded, and her eyes traveled up and down Gwen's form. "I'm sure I have something that will suffice. About an eight, is that right?"

"Yes, or ten sometimes." Gwen's voice was soft and aimed at the floor. Was she embarrassed? Drew couldn't care less what size she was, but he knew body image was something most women struggled with.

"Follow me," Claire said and led the way toward the

back corner of the store. Drew followed until he noticed the fitting room area. Two large armchairs sat facing an open area with three long mirrors that he assumed was where the woman could model the clothing. He parked himself in one of the chairs and waited.

A few minutes later, Claire opened a dressing room for Gwen and hung up several dresses. "There's a small mirror inside, but if you like the way they look, you can step out and view it in the longer mirrors." She pointed to the open area.

"Thank you." Gwen closed the dressing room door and Drew waited. When she emerged, his breath caught in his throat. The black dress hugged her in all the right places and flared out at the hips. The neckline was black lace. "What do you think?" she asked twirling for him.

"It's beautiful," Drew said. In fact, he wasn't sure he had ever seen such a beautiful vision before.

"Shall I even try the others?"

Though he couldn't imagine one looking any better, Drew encouraged her to model the rest. He was not only curious to see how they would look, but he was taking mental notes on dresses he could buy her in the future. The other four dresses looked stunning as well, but nothing compared to the first one.

"Do you have any jewelry to complement the dress?" Claire asked.

"I didn't bring any," Gwen said shaking her head.

"Do you have any here?" Drew asked.

"Drew, I couldn't-"

"You can," Drew said, grabbing her hand. "The outfit

needs it." He lowered his voice and leaned closer to her ear. "Princess, remember?" Gwen nodded, but Drew wondered if he was pushing it. He didn't want to scare her off by pushing his money on her either. "Just a pair of earrings though, I think."

Claire nodded and motioned them to follow her to the other side of the store. The jewelry collection wasn't large, but the pieces were extraordinary. Claire scanned the offerings before plucking off a dainty pair of onyx earrings. "These would look lovely."

"We'll take them," Drew said.

Gwen was quiet as Claire rang up the purchases. She gripped her bag tightly which now held her casual clothes and tennis shoes along with her robe, and her eyes remained on the floor. Drew handed over his platinum card, signed the slip without a second thought, and thanked Claire before taking Gwen's hand again.

As they stepped outside, he turned to her. "I'm sorry. I wanted to spoil you, but I have the feeling I've made you uncomfortable."

Gwen smiled up at him. "A little I suppose. It's wonderful that you have so much money, but I don't live like this. I live paycheck to paycheck and work two jobs. This dress and earrings costs a month's pay if not more. I just...."

Drew pulled her hands to his chest. "Gwen, I'm so sorry. You are amazing, and I wanted to show you that."

"You don't have to spend so much money to show me that. Money is important, Drew, but it's not everything, and it could help so many people who need it." She took a deep breath and looked down.

Drew moved a hand to push her chin back up. "I've lived a privileged life, Gwen, but I'd like to be the man you're looking for. Help me learn."

Her gaze penetrated his, and he poured his emotion into his gaze. If the eyes were windows to the soul, he wanted her to read his honesty.

"Okay." Her voice was soft and breathy and though he wasn't sure she would be receptive, Drew couldn't fight the magnetic pull that lowered his head until his lips touched hers.

Heat flared between them and raced down his spine warming his body from the inside. His heartbeat doubled as if shot with amphetamine. When the kiss ended, he could tell it had affected Gwen just as much. Her breath was labored, and she blinked rapidly at him. "Sorry, I've wanted to do that since the masquerade ball."

"Me too."

*A*s they rode back in the jet that evening, Drew stole glances at Gwen from the corner of his eye. After the kiss, they had walked around town for a time before their reservation for dinner. While he had wanted to buy more for her, he had refrained. It would be challenging, but he was determined to be the man she needed.

She was so unlike any woman he had ever dated. Even

Avery, who claimed she didn't want a billionaire boyfriend, had wanted him to buy things for her. But Gwen truly acted as if money meant nothing to her. It gave Drew pause. Perhaps he was putting too much emphasis on money as well.

"So, tell me about your church," he said turning to her. "I mean what should I expect?"

Gwen's eyes lit up. "Well, it's very welcoming. Someone will greet you at the front door with a smile. Probably shake your hand too. Then they'll hand you a bulletin which details events happening during the week, and we will go in and have a seat."

"That doesn't sound bad so far," he said though meeting new people always set him a little on edge. It came with having money. He constantly had to decide if they liked him for him or for what they hoped to get from him.

"Then there's music," Gwen continued. "It's mostly contemporary though somehow I doubt you listen to Christian radio."

He interrupted her with a smile, "No? What kind of music do you think I listen to?"

She cocked her head as she studied him. "Hmm, I think I'd take you more for a rock 'n' roll kind of guy."

"Guilty." Drew was more a fan of rock music but the oldies like AC/DC or Kiss.

"And then the preacher will speak. His sermon usually lasts thirty to forty-five minutes and then he'll close in prayer. Sometimes we sing a closing song before he releases us. All in all, it's only about an hour of your life, but if you come with an open heart, I can pretty much guarantee it'll be the best hour of your week."

Drew wasn't sure about that. But Gwen had something he found he was missing, and if that something was God, he was willing to take a chance to see.

"I'm looking forward to it," he said.

CHAPTER 12

Gwen woke the next morning before her alarm clock. Drew would attend her church today, and she hoped he enjoyed it. As much fun as she had last night, Gwen knew Drew would have to be a believer before she could become serious with him. She wanted to get married and have a family but only with someone who would love and serve the Lord as much as she did.

Gwen kicked back the covers and padded to the bathroom for a shower. Ten minutes later, she stood in her closet surveying her wardrobe. There was nothing wrong with any of it, but she felt more pressure to look nice today knowing Drew would be there. After debating back and forth, she decided on a simple skirt and sweater. The hunter green color brought out the sparkle in her eyes and the copper in her hair.

Satisfied with her appearance, Gwen headed to the kitchen to make breakfast and coffee. Drew would pick her up in half an hour, and she didn't want to still be shoveling food in when he arrived.

The knock at her door arrived just as she was getting the bacon out of the fridge. This time she didn't wait; she hurried to the door in case it was another threat. It was too early to be Drew, and she wasn't expecting anyone else.

She flung the door open and stared in surprise when Drew's face greeted her from the other side. "You're early." Gwen hadn't meant the words to come out like an accusation, but it was clear from his raised brow that they had landed that way.

"Should I go then?" He turned to walk away, but Gwen caught the smile on his face. He was teasing her.

"No." She grabbed his arm to stop him and a tingle shot up her arm. "I just haven't eaten yet is all."

"Good, I was hoping to catch you before you did. I have breakfast waiting in the car, and I was hoping you would join me."

"Eat in the limo?"

"Why not? It's not pancakes or waffles, so you won't have to worry about syrup." His blue eyes danced.

"All right, let me put the bacon away. Lucky for you, I hadn't started the coffee yet." She couldn't believe how easy it was to joke around with him.

"You wouldn't have come with me if you had?" His face pulled into a forlorn expression. "I see how I rate."

Gwen just laughed. She loved how he made her feel lighter. "Just let me grab my Bible and purse." *And a stick of gum* she thought to herself as she wouldn't get to brush her teeth after breakfast now.

She dashed into the kitchen and stashed the bacon back in the fridge. Then she rummaged in her drawers until she found a pack of gum. She didn't chew it often, but she tried to keep some around just for moments like these.

Gum in hand, she grabbed her purse, slipping it in, and then her Bible and journal off the table where she had been about to do her devotional. "Okay, I'm ready."

Drew held out his arm, and Gwen slipped her hand through it enjoying the strong essence of masculinity and security from him.

As they climbed into the limo, she was surprised by the smell of eggs and bacon. Drew had said it wasn't pancakes or waffles but trying to eat eggs in the car might be just as messy at least if they landed on her outfit. "Eggs?" she asked as he shut the door.

A crooked smile alighted on his lips. "Egg burritos. The best in the city." He opened a compartment near the fridge and pulled out two large tin foil cylinders.

"This is enormous," Gwen said with a laugh as he passed one to her.

"And delicious. My mother hates that I eat these, but I'm addicted."

Gwen glanced at him as she unwrapped one side of her monstrosity. The comment about his mother had caught her attention as it wasn't the first time he had said something about her disapproval. "Your mother isn't a fan of some of your habits?"

Drew snorted. "Not at all. My mother is the epitome of the wealthy elite. One must always eat healthy, dress appropriately, and never cause a scene."

Gwen's heart ached for him. It was clear from his words that he and his mother had a rocky relationship and while that was better than no relationship at all like she had, it was still challenging. "That must be difficult."

"That's one word for it, but let's not discuss my mother. Let's enjoy the wonderful food, the company," he winked at her, "and the ride."

Gwen wanted to say more, but it was clear from his words that he was finished with the conversation, so she finished unwrapping her burrito and took a bite. It was delicious. Eggs, bacon, and cheese mixed together to create an explosion of flavors in her mouth. It was the best egg burrito she had ever eaten. Drew was full of surprises.

*D*rew's bravado faded as they pulled into the parking lot of the church. He disliked situations where he didn't feel in control, and this qualified. There were too many unknown variables. He didn't know the people, the procedure, or the layout. All things he versed himself in before attending new venues.

"You ready?" Gwen's voice was soft and encouraging beside him.

He flashed what he hoped was a confident smile. "As I'll ever be, I suppose."

Manuel opened the door, and Drew stepped out first then held his hand to Gwen. He hoped she wouldn't mind, but he laced his fingers through hers. This was her place and she exuded a feeling of confidence that he needed.

As she had said, a friendly couple greeted them at the door and handed them a bulletin. Drew smiled and nodded but made no attempt at small talk. It wasn't his forte anyway and certainly not when he felt less than confident.

He let Gwen lead the way into the sanctuary and sat beside her. Three large screens hung behind the stage which was filled with instruments. The large room could probably seat three hundred though Drew doubted even half that amount was there currently. "Does it usually fill up?" he asked her quietly as his eyes scoped the area for exits. Not that he expected a scene, but it was always nice to know the quickest way out of a building in case.

She shook her head. "There are two services. The first one is larger, maybe two hundred most weeks. I'd say this one is half that. Maybe a little more."

That made him feel better. At least there wouldn't be a huge crowd if something did unfold. A minute later, several people stepped onto the stage and the music began. It wasn't rock, but Drew could appreciate the talent of the people playing. He had never heard the songs, but he enjoyed listening to Gwen sing beside him. Her voice was soft but clear, and occasionally, her eyes would close as she sang. She looked peaceful as if the rest of the world didn't matter.

"This next song is new," the worship leader said, "and it has powerful words. If you'll let me, I'd like to personalize the words and read them over you. If you're comfortable with it, please close your eyes and listen."

The woman began to read in a clear voice, but the words meant little to Drew. At least until she reached the chorus. "... The love of God chases you down, fights till you're found, leaves the ninety-nine. You didn't earn it, and you don't deserve it, but still He gives Himself away..." The woman continued but Drew's ears stopped listening. He didn't know what the ninety-nine were, and he was having trouble grappling with him not deserving it. While not a believer, Drew felt he was a decent person. He donated to charities, he hired those he could, and he had done nothing truly terrible. Why wasn't that enough for God?

The pastor's message didn't seem to address the lyrics, and Drew knew he would have to ask Gwen about them after the service.

"What did you think?" Gwen asked him when the final song ended, and people began exiting the church.

"I have questions," he said. "Do you have time for lunch?"

Gwen squeezed his hand and offered a smile. "Of course."

Half an hour later, they parked at a viewpoint in the city. Drew had opted to grab fast food and eat in the car, so they wouldn't be interrupted.

"So, what's your question?" Gwen asked as she opened the Styrofoam container. The salty smell of soy sauce reached Drew's nose, and his stomach rumbled.

"It's about that song the woman read. She said 'you don't

deserve it' but I'm a good person, Gwen. How could I not deserve it?" He took a bite of his noodles as he waited for her response.

"It isn't about being a good person, Drew. God says that 'by Grace are you saved through faith, and that not of yourself, it is the gift of God, not of good works lest any man should boast'. It's not about doing good things. It's about letting God into your life."

"So, the only way to receive God's love is by letting him into my life?" That sounded like a piece of control that Drew wasn't sure he could relinquish.

"You already have God's love, Drew. There's nothing you could do to make Him love you more than he loves you right now. He's just waiting for you to want a relationship with Him."

"But a relationship with Him requires changing my life, right?"

Gwen smiled. "Well, when you accept Jesus into your life, you want to live differently. I don't feel like I'm missing out on anything, and I couldn't imagine living any other way."

Drew let that sink in. Gwen had something he was missing in his life, but he wasn't sure he was ready to give up control.

CHAPTER 13

"*H*ow come you have returned none of my calls, Drew?"

Drew glanced up at Avery who stood leaning in his doorway. "I was on a date, Avery. It would have been rude to answer your calls on a date." Suddenly, he remembered the flowers and the note in his car. He needed to stop by and see Scott this afternoon.

Avery sashayed into the room. "With Gwen?"

"Yes, with Gwen. Who else would it be with?"

Avery tilted her head and crossed her slender arms. "You should be careful, Drew. You will only break her heart."

Drew blinked at her. This was a new side of Avery and one he didn't like very much. "And why is that?"

"Because you're from two different worlds. It will never work out."

"That's ridiculous and antiquated thinking. There have

been plenty of relationships where one party was poorer than the other that worked."

Avery shrugged. "It didn't work for me. I'm just trying to save you both some heartbreak."

"What do you mean?" Drew asked. "I thought you came back because you were broke."

With an exaggerated sigh, Avery plopped down in the chair across from him. "I did, but I became broke because of this guy I met. He was amazing, or so I thought. Poor, but charming. Turned out he was a con artist and was siphoning my money away right under my nose."

"Avery, I'm sorry that happened, but Gwen isn't like that. I ran a background check on her. She might be poor, but she's no thief."

"You're probably right." Avery flicked her hair off her shoulders. "Have you told your mother yet?"

"No, I'm still working on that, but I will soon. I'd appreciate it if you didn't tell her either."

Avery held up her hands. "I'm not going to say anything. So, how about lunch?"

"I'd love to, but I've got an errand to run. Maybe we can do lunch another time."

"All right, I'll try to find a hole in your schedule, so we can meet up."

Drew did not miss the hint of hurt in her voice. He felt bad, but he needed to go see Scott before he was off work. When he was sure Avery was gone, he texted Manuel, grabbed his coat, and headed out of the building.

"Back so soon?" Scott asked as Drew crossed the room.

"I know I'm out of favors, but I need one anyway."

Scott raised a brow. "Okay, but it's going cost you a bigger donation this year."

"Understood, and I'll be happy to."

Scott's eyes dropped to the bundle in Drew's hands. "Fine, follow me." He led the way to the office again and pulled the door shut. "What is it this time?"

"It's these." Drew set the flowers and the note on the coffee table. "The girl, the one I asked you to run the background check on, she got them delivered to her apartment before our date yesterday. It's not much, probably a prank, but I was hoping you could dust them for prints. Mine will be on there and hers too."

"What does the card say?" Scott asked.

"Cinderella wasn't real. I know it seems silly," Drew continued when Scott raised a brow, "but she's had a hard life and she spooks easily. I just don't want to ignore this, and have it turn out to be something bigger."

"All right, I'll see what I can do, but I wasn't kidding about that check, my friend."

"It will be in the mail, I promise. Just let me know when you have anything."

*G*wen sighed as she stared at the mountain of papers in front of her. She was trying to stay focused, but memories of the last few evenings with Drew kept flooding her vision. It had been less than two weeks since she'd met him, but she already felt herself falling for this guy and that scared her. The only thing that gave her pause was his faith. He hadn't committed his heart to God, but he had agreed to come to church with her again.

A glance at the clock revealed she was out of time. Drew was taking her to some benefit tonight and she needed to get to Carrie's to find a dress and get her hair done. Drew had offered to buy her a dress, but Gwen didn't feel right about taking his money until they were more serious. The last thing she needed was to have him buy her a ton of gifts and then they break up for some reason. She would never get over the guilt.

With a final look at her papers - she'd have to come in early tomorrow - she packed up her things and headed out.

"How are things with your Prince Charming?"

Gwen sighed as Tom's voice reached her. It had been a quiet week with no hounding from him, and she had hoped it would stay that way. Then his words sank in. She whirled to face him. "What did you say?"

"I asked how things are with your Prince Charming."

Fear flooded Gwen and her knees began to shake. Had she been wrong about the sender of the flowers? Or was it just a coincidence he had called Drew Prince Charming? She didn't want to stay to find out. "I have to go." She turned and sprinted to her car.

When she was safely in the car with her doors locked, she allowed herself a moment to close her eyes and calm her breathing. She wouldn't be able to concentrate with her heart pounding like a snare drum out of her chest, and she didn't want to risk getting in an accident. Thankfully, Tom hadn't followed her and a few minutes later, she was able to turn the ignition.

"What happened to you?" Carrie asked as Gwen stepped inside.

"You remember the flowers and the note I told you about?"

Carrie's nose wrinkled. "The creepy black ones?"

"Yeah, well Tom, this guy at work who keeps asking me out, asked me how my Prince Charming was."

"Maybe it was just a coincidence," Carrie said, "but I agree that sounds creepy. Try to put it out of your mind though. You've got a benefit to get ready for."

"You're right." But it was easier said than done. If her stalker turned out to be Tom, what was she going to do about it?

CHAPTER 14

*D*rew smiled when Gwen opened the door. Her emerald green gown showed off her porcelain skin, and her red hair was pulled up on her head in an artistic up do. "You look beautiful," he said.

"Thanks. It's a little tight, but I think I'll be okay. Just don't let me eat too much." She patted her stomach in a self-conscious gesture.

"Gwen, I would have bought you a dress that fits."

"I know, Drew, but I don't feel right accepting such extravagant gifts until-"

"Until you're sure about us?" he supplied.

A sheepish grin stole across her face. "I'm sorry-"

"Don't be. I understand. Thank you, Carrie, for the dress," he said to Carrie as she entered the living room.

"My pleasure anytime, Drew."

"You sure you don't want to go with us? I'm sure I could get you in."

Carrie flicked her hand. "Thanks for the invite, Drew, but I have a date with Raphael tonight."

Gwen chuckled and rolled her eyes. "Come on, let's go."

"All right. Have fun then." Drew took Gwen's hand and led her outside. "Is Raphael the one she skipped the ball for?" he asked as the front door closed behind them.

Gwen smiled. "No, that was Lorenzo, but I honestly couldn't tell you who Raphael is. Carrie's what I like to call a serial dater. I love her, but I don't always understand her."

"Well, I'm glad you don't take after her." He held the limo door open and helped her slide in.

"Me too."

His phone chimed as the limo door shut. It was Scott. While he normally wouldn't answer the phone on a date, this one concerned Gwen too, so he flashed an apologetic smile and tapped the button. "Hey Scott, you find anything out?"

"I'm afraid not, Drew. There were prints but only yours and Gwen's. I'm sure it's nothing to worry about, but if she gets anything else, let me know."

"Thanks, Scott." Drew swallowed his frustration and ended the call. "Sorry about that. It was my friend, the police officer. I was hoping he had information about your flowers, but he couldn't find any usable fingerprints."

"That's all right. I think it might be the guy at my work after all. He asked about my Prince Charming today."

A knot formed in Drew's stomach. He didn't like anyone threatening Gwen and certainly not at her job where he had little control. "Would you like me to speak to him?"

"No, that would probably make it worse. I think he'll let it go, eventually."

Drew wasn't sure about that - he'd had his fair share of stalkers and they rarely stopped of their own accord - but he let it go. He didn't want to ruin the evening.

❀

*G*wen grabbed Drew's hand as she stepped out of the limo. Even though she was here with him, attending this gala still terrified her. What if they didn't let her in? What if she made a fool of herself or him? A camera flashed, and Gwen jumped and curled closer to Drew.

"Drew, who's the new girl?" the man behind the camera asked.

"Don't worry about them," Drew whispered in her ear. "Just ignore and keep walking."

"Oh, come on, Drew, just a name?"

The man was relentless, and Gwen sighed with relief when they were safely in the building and away from the man with the camera. "Will that be printed?"

"It's hard to say. We never know when they take pictures which ones they are going to use, but it's a possibility. Don't worry, you look beautiful though."

Gwen wasn't worried about her appearance. What she was worried about was her privacy. She couldn't imagine her school would be too excited if reporters showed up there looking for her. And what if they looked her up? She didn't need her past being splashed across the headlines. What had she been thinking? "Drew, I don't know-"

Before she could finish, a woman's voice called out to them. "Drew, Gwen, over here." Avery waved to them from the doorway of a large room.

Beside her, she felt Drew stiffen, and Gwen wondered why. She had thought he and Avery were friends.

"I was hoping you two would come." Avery was stunning in her low cut floor-length gown. It sparkled as the light caught it. "Gwen, you look absolutely radiant."

Gwen didn't know Avery well enough to discern if she was telling the truth or just being nice, so she gave her the benefit of the doubt. "Thank you, Avery. You do as well."

"Oh pish," Avery said with a wave of her hand. "Come on, we're seated at the same table." She turned and led the way to the table. Gwen didn't miss the slight swinging of her hips, and she glanced at Drew to see if he was watching, but his facial features were pulled tight and his eyes stared straight ahead.

Avery sat down at the table and pointed to the seats next to her. Drew's name was on a card directly on Avery 's left, and Gwen's name was on a card next to Drew. On Gwen's left was a woman's name. "Who's Jacqueline?" she asked.

"My mother," Drew said with a pinched smile.

Gwen's heart dropped like a lead weight. She had never met the woman and now she would have to sit next to her all evening? As if the very thought had summoned her, a thin woman with graying hair strode their direction.

"Avery, it's so good to see you again," the woman said as

she picked up and squeezed Avery's hands. "And you got Drew to say yes? Good for you."

"Actually, Mother, I'm here with Gwen." Drew spoke up. His arm slipped around Gwen's waist, and he pulled her closer to him.

Gwen was thankful for the support as Jacqueline's eyes raked over her in a disapproving glance.

"And just who is Gwen?"

"She's the woman from the masquerade ball, Mother."

"I thought you said her name was Carrie."

"It was a simple misunderstanding," Drew said. "This is Gwen Rodgers."

"I see. And what do you do, Gwen?"

Gwen swallowed. Drew's mother was terrifying. Though beautiful, her eyes flashed daggers into Gwen, and her posture was so straight Gwen wondered if a rod had been attached to her spine. "Um, I'm a teacher."

Jacqueline's eyes shifted to Drew as her brow arched. "And just how did a teacher get invited to my ball?"

"Gwen also manages charitable donations for some rather large companies," Drew said. "Perhaps that is how she was invited." That wasn't the truth - she only managed donations for his company - but Gwen knew better than to contradict him.

"I see." Her eyes bore holes into Gwen, and she licked her lips as if she was going to say something else. "Well, I look forward to getting to know you, Gwen."

Gwen doubted that, but she flashed a tight-lipped smile at the woman. Nice. She could be nice. She might have to remind herself that this woman was a child of God as well. A lot. But she could be nice.

Drew squeezed her waist and leaned in close. His breath tickled her ear as he whispered. "Don't let her get to you."

Gwen appreciated the encouraging words, but she had no doubt his mother was out to make her night miserable. Drew pulled out her chair, and she took her seat thankful that a glass of water was in front of her. Her throat was already parched. As she reached for the glass though, her hand slipped, and she sent the glass crashing against the table. Water spilled out across the table pooling towards Avery and Jacqueline as if it knew exactly who would hate it the most.

"Oh my gosh, I'm so sorry." Gwen stood to search for a napkin and her sudden ascent knocked her chair over. Her chair crashed to the ground causing Gwen to jump. And of course, she couldn't jump Drew's direction. No, she had to jump Jacqueline's direction. Jacqueline had just picked up her own water glass and Gwen just barely bumped her arm, but it was enough to send the water spraying out of the top and all over Jacqueline.

"Well, I never."

Gwen's eyes widened, and her heart exploded into a trillion tiny pieces. His mother would never like her now. Recovering slightly, she grabbed a napkin off the table behind them and tried to dab at Jacqueline's dress.

"Young lady, stop. You have done quite enough, and I am capable of drying myself off."

Gwen dropped the napkin and stepped back. "Of

course, ma'am, I'm so sorry." She looked to Drew who had managed to keep his wits about him and was sopping up the table. "I'm so sorry." Then she fled for the door before the hot tears building up behind her eyes could spill down her cheeks. She had let Carrie help with her makeup and she didn't need to add insult to injury by staying as tears created black trails of mascara down her cheeks.

She didn't stop running until she burst through the front door. Too late she remembered the photographer. Camera bulbs flashed in her face and his voice carried to her. "Excuse me, are you the woman with Drew Devonshire? Did he break up with you? Hit you?"

Oh crud, she had leaped right out of the frying pan and into the fire. They might not have used her picture before, but she had just given them interesting fodder. She pulled the door open behind her and stepped back into the building. It was safer inside right now though that wasn't saying much. She turned, hoping to find a corner to hide in, but found herself against a solid chest instead. Gwen knew it was Drew before her eyes reached his face.

"Why did you run?" His hands clasped her arms, not tightly but with enough force that she couldn't bolt again.

"Are you kidding me?" She sniffed. "I made a mess in there."

"Yeah, you did."

She gaped at him wondering how he could be so cruel, and then his lip twitched. Merriment flickered in his eyes. "It was great."

"How can you say that? It was mortifying."

He pursed his lips together, but she could see his shoulders moving just slightly. He was laughing. At her. "It's not funny, Drew."

"Actually, it is, Gwen. These benefits are always so stuffy. I hate coming to them, but this one...this one will go down in the books."

"Yeah, but not in a good way." Gwen had known it would be hard to win over his mother, but now she was fairly certain that door was closed for good. And though she wasn't dating his mother, having the woman hate her would put a strain on any kind of relationship they might have. "And why did you invite me if you hate these things?"

Drew shrugged. "Because I'm supposed to be here and coming with you at least made the thought of the night bearable."

"Drew, maybe you need a woman like Avery. I'm not cut out for events like this. I'll only keep embarrassing you."

"Hey." He let go of her left arm to place a finger under her chin. "I don't need a woman like Avery. I needed a reason not to go to these stuffy events and now I have one. In fact, let's get out of here."

"Have you lost your mind? Your mother will kill you if you leave, and that reporter outside already saw me and thinks we broke up or you hit me or something."

A mischievous gleam appeared in Drew's eyes. "Then let's really give him something to talk about."

Before she could say anything more, he opened the door and pulled her out with him. As expected, the cameras flashed, but Drew said nothing. Instead, he turned to her, circled his arms around her waist, and pulled her in for a kiss.

Gwen was so shocked that she stood as still as a statue for a moment, but the heat from his lips traveled through her body, and with a mind of their own, her arms wound around his neck. She could hear clicks, but she was no longer sure they were from the cameras because it felt like fireworks were exploding all around her.

Too soon he pulled back. "Come on, let's go get some S'mores."

"What?" She looked up at him still dazed from the kiss, but he didn't answer. He tightened his grip on her hand and pulled. With his other hand, he retrieved his phone and hollered for Manuel to meet them at the corner.

He must have been close by because the limo pulled up just as they reached the end of the block. Without waiting for Manuel to open the door, Drew yanked it open and piled in after her. "Drive," he shouted to Manuel and the limo sped off.

CHAPTER 15

"This is where you live?" Gwen asked. Her eyes widened like saucers as the limo pulled up to a palatial estate. The mansion looked as if it took up an entire city block. She could count at least three chimneys and a four-car garage.

Drew's lips twitched into a smile, and his dimple popped out. "Yes, this is home. It's a little much for just me."

"I'll say." The words tumbled out of Gwen's mouth before she could stop them. "I'm sorry. That was rude."

"Perhaps, but it's the truth. I didn't want such a large place, but my mother insisted I take it over when my father died. She moved to a smaller place in the city thinking I would fill it with a family, but I haven't accomplished that yet."

"Do you want to? Fill it with a family?" Why was she asking such personal questions? Except she knew the answer. She wanted to know everything about him.

His eyes caught hers and Gwen's breath stilled as the flood of emotion emanating from him hit her.

"Yes, I hope one day to marry and have kids."

"Have you ever been close?" Gwen wasn't sure why she cared, but a part of her felt compelled to know. How many women had been in his past? How many close enough to marry?

Drew nodded, "I was close once. Her name was Marjorie, and I thought she was attracted to me rather than my money. However, shortly after I proposed, she ran away with my chauffeur."

Gwen's eyes widened, and her hand flew to her mouth. "I'm so sorry. That's awful."

"It was, but I'm glad I found out who she was before I married her. What about you? Were you ever close?"

Gwen's smile was wistful. "I was once. I'm sure you understand that with my past, it's hard for me to let people in, but Adam made it past all my walls. He was charming and said all the right things to a girl who needed to hear them. I'm not sure why he even proposed to me because it turned out he was having an affair with his secretary."

Drew's blue eyes softened in sympathy. "Gwen, I'm sorry. I'm sure that didn't help your trust issues."

She sniffed and bit the inside of her lip. Her head shook slightly. Help them? It made them nearly insurmountable. "I should have known better though. Adam attended church with me, but I could tell he wasn't a believer. He was just going through the motions, but I kept telling myself he just needed a little longer." Gwen stopped as she realized she could be talking about Drew as well.

Drew opened his mouth as if he were about to say something, but before he could, the limo pulled to a stop. "Hungry?" He asked with a lopsided smile.

Gwen's stomach rumbled in answer, and a sheepish grin stole across her face as her hands covered her traitorous belly. "I guess so."

"Let's go then." He grabbed the grocery bag full of marshmallows, chocolate, and graham crackers they had stopped at the store to get and stepped out of the limo.

His backyard was expansive. Not that she would have expected any less. A gazebo sat near the house and overlooked both a pond and a swimming pool. Near it was a fire pit with several chairs and beyond that was a grassy area and a tennis court.

"Are you cold?" he asked. "I could send Manuel to get a coat while I start the fire."

A shiver raced across her shoulders and Gwen nodded. She hadn't realized she was cold, but that was because the limo had been so toasty.

"Manuel, can you fetch a jacket for Gwen?"

Manuel issued a nod and raced off toward the house. Gwen followed Drew over to the fire pit. There were already logs in the fire pit and near it, a small chest. Drew opened it to reveal matches, lighter fluid, and metal rods. A few minutes later, he had a roaring fire going.

Gwen inhaled the smoky air. Her foster parents had

taken her camping once, and it was one of her favorite memories. There was something about watching the flames of the fire dance. Beautiful and deadly.

"Ready for S'mores?" Drew asked. He had already set out the graham crackers and broken up the chocolate on a nearby table.

"I've never had them," Gwen said with a shrug.

Drew's eyes bulged. "What? How could you have never had S'mores? They're like an American staple."

"I've only been camping once and unlike you, my friends at college didn't hang out at bonfires." That was because she hadn't had many friends at college. And even after she and Carrie had become friends that hadn't been Carrie's idea of a fun Friday night.

"Well, then I'm glad I get to be here for your first experience."

Manuel arrived then with a jacket, and Gwen slipped her arms in thankful for the extra heat.

"Now, the trick is that you warm the marshmallow before you blacken it, so that the inside is nice and gooey." Drew held a silver rod out to her with a marshmallow shoved on the end of it. Gwen took the rod and turned to the fire.

"Like this?"

Drew filled the space behind her and his hand guided her arm to a slightly higher position. "Here," he said. His lips were close to her ear and Gwen had to focus to keep her arm from shaking. Just the nearness of his body was sending tremors through hers.

They stood that way for a minute, then he dipped her arm down. "Now, we blacken it just slightly." The marshmallow caught fire and Gwen gasped, but Drew simply pulled back on her arm and blew the flame out like a candle on a cake. "Now, sandwich it between the crackers and chocolate."

Gwen hurried to the table and placed the marshmallow on a graham cracker with chocolate. Then she used the top graham cracker to hold it in place while she pulled the rod out. When the rod was clear, the marshmallow squished, and white goo trickled out the sides of the miniature sandwich. She brought it to her mouth and took a bite.

"Mm, this is delicious," she said, her mouth full of the concoction.

The corners of Drew's lips curled up and his eyes crinkled. "You're enjoying that, huh?"

Gwen nodded and took another bite. How had she never had these before? They were like the perfect little dessert. Delicious and handheld.

"I can see that," he said taking a step closer to her. "Want to know how I know?"

Gwen swallowed her bite. His tone had changed from playful to a deep, sexy tone. His hand reached out and touched the corner of her lip. "I can see the evidence on your face."

He wiped slightly and showed Gwen the white residue on his finger, but she couldn't speak. Her eyes were fixed on him. He took another step toward her, and before she could say a word, his lips found hers. They were sweet and hungry at the same time. The remainder of her cracker fell to the ground as her arms wound around his neck, and Gwen felt herself falling. Oh boy was she in trouble.

CHAPTER 16

"**W**hy do you smell like smoke?" Carrie asked as Gwen floated past her into the living room. "No, not just smoke, you smell like a campfire. Why do you smell like a campfire?"

"Because we had S'mores." Gwen couldn't wipe the goofy smile from her face. Her cheeks felt glued in a perpetual grin.

"S'mores? I thought you were going to a benefit." Carrie crossed her arms and leaned against her counter. "All right, spill it."

"It was amazing," Gwen said with a sigh and then blinked to focus. "I mean not at first. The benefit was scary. Everyone was perfect and important, and I spilled water on the table. Then I spilled water on his mother."

"Wait, you met his mother?"

"Yeah, and she hates me. I tried to mop up the water I

spilled on her. Then I ran out, but Drew followed me, and he kissed me for the cameras."

"What cameras?" Carrie asked.

Gwen shrugged. "I don't know. Some reporter. Then we ran. We ran to the limo and drove to the grocery store."

"The grocery store? Gwen, did you have special brownies or something?"

Gwen laughed. "No, we bought marshmallows, graham crackers, and chocolate. Then he took me back to his place. It's huge, Carrie, and he made a fire and we roasted S'mores."

"I think toasted is the proper word."

"It was amazing."

"You made S'mores instead of going to the benefit? Who is this guy?"

Gwen had an answer for that. He was her idea of a perfect man, but she would not say that out loud yet. She didn't want to jinx it, so she changed the subject. "I'm sorry about your dress. It might be a little dirty, but I'll pay for the dry cleaning."

Carrie smiled. "I don't care about the dress. I'm just glad to see you smiling."

Gwen was glad too. She hadn't known how lonely she was until tonight. Over S'mores and a crackling fire, she and Drew had opened up to each other. She'd told him about her past and her insecurities with men. He'd told her about his desire to do something more noble than run hotels.

"What are you going to do?" she asked.

"I will tell her I'm leaving. I'll stay until I can train someone else, probably until the end of the year, but then I'm leaving. Tonight made me realize that life is too short to do something you hate. You made me realize that." He pulled her closer to him and wrapped his arm around her shoulder.

"Drew, I don't want to the be the cause for you leaving the family business."

"You aren't. I haven't been happy for a while, but I couldn't place my finger on why. Until tonight. I miss this. I miss relaxing with friends and chatting by the fire. My life is meetings and hotels now, and that's not a life."

"Okay, Cheshire cat, you're staying here tonight."

"What? No, I'm okay," Gwen said. "I need to get back to Tabby."

"Tabby will be fine. I've been trying to get your attention for three minutes. You cannot drive. You're a risk. I've never seen anyone so high on life they couldn't drive, but that is definitely you."

Gwen wanted to protest, but Carrie was right. She hadn't heard her friend and her focus was on the last few hours and nothing more. "Okay, you win, but I don't have any pajamas."

Carrie smiled. "I've got you covered as long as you promise not to smoke them out too."

rew was just about to retire for the evening when Pierre appeared at his door. "I'm sorry to bother

you, sir, but your mother is downstairs, and she will not take no for an answer."

Drew sighed. He had known his mother would want to talk to him, but he hadn't been expecting her so soon. "Tell her I'll be right there, Pierre."

He grabbed his robe as Pierre left the room and flung it about his shoulders. There was no way he wanted to have a conversation with his mother in his sleepwear. The robe wasn't much better, but it was something.

"Are you happy?" She accosted him before he made it to the bottom of the stairs. "You've made us the laughingstock of the town!" His mother shoved a phone in his face and Drew glanced at the headline. *Billionaire Blows off Charitable Event.* Underneath was a picture of Gwen and him running toward the limo. Well, at least they hadn't used the one of her crying. He had been worried about that headline. This? This was manageable.

"Wow, that was fast."

"Of course it was, Drew. This is the information age. They don't have to wait to print it when they can throw it up on the internet where it lives forever."

"Mother, you are being dramatic. I didn't blow off the benefit. I attended. I just left early."

"You left before it began with that hooligan you brought."

A spark of anger flared in Drew and he folded his arms across his chest. "She is not a hooligan, Mother. She is a perfectly nice girl who got nervous. Perhaps if you had been nicer to her, she might not have been so skittish."

"It is not my job to placate your playthings-"

"She is not a plaything, Mother. She is a hardworking, honest teacher, and I care for her."

"You've only been seeing her a few weeks," his mother said in a dismissive tone as if the conversation was finished.

"Those few weeks have been long enough. She's real, Mother, and she made me realize what I was missing. I hate those benefits and galas and balls. I'm not Father. I'm not cut out to be the face of the Devonshire hotel chain, and I've decided I'm not going to do it anymore."

"What?" Her eyes narrowed to tiny slits.

"I'll stay until the new year. That will give me plenty of time to train someone else, but then I'm stepping down. I don't want to keep doing this."

"You would turn your back on family?"

"I'm not turning my back on you, Mother. I'm simply following my heart."

"Well, hopefully your heart doesn't bankrupt our family." With a final pointed look, she whirled and strode out of his house.

Drew sighed. He had known his mother would take it hard, but he hadn't quite expected that reaction.

CHAPTER 17

*D*rew was surprised to find his mother in his office when he returned from his errand. It had been three weeks since their discussion at his house and she hadn't spoken to him once in that time. What could she want now?

"Hello, Mother. To what do I owe this pleasure?"

His mother rose from his chair and walked around the desk. "I've been thinking, Drew, that perhaps I've been too hard on you. You should do what you want with your life and spend it with whom you want."

Drew cocked his head but said nothing. He didn't know where this was going yet.

"I'm going to hate losing you from the family business, but I am pleased with the man you've hired to replace you."

"Thank you." Drew didn't dare say more until he could discern her motive for being here.

"But I have one favor to ask of you."

And there it was.

"There's a charity benefit tonight. I'd like you to attend. It will be your last one."

Drew shook his head. "Sorry, Mother, I have a date with Gwen tonight."

His mother's lips pulled into a tight smile. "I don't think I was clear, Drew. If you want to keep your fortune, you will attend this last benefit tonight. Alone."

"I can't cancel on such short notice, Mother. It would be rude, and haven't you always prided yourself on not being rude?"

Her smile widened, but it didn't reach her eyes. "Of course, I wouldn't want you to be rude. That's why I purchased two spa packages. Avery is going to take her out tonight. She can get all relaxed for your date tomorrow."

Drew's eyes narrowed. Was it possible his mother was being nice to Gwen? Somehow, he doubted it. "Why is it so important she isn't at the benefit tonight, Mother? I could just tell her we had to change our plans and bring her."

"No offense, dear, but I remember the way she behaved last time. This is an important benefit. One that could set us up with some new investors, but only if everything goes smoothly, if you get my drift."

Drew got her insinuation all right. Gwen wasn't welcome because she might screw things up. He didn't want to be there either, but he had been spending the last few days trying to figure out how he'd live if his mother cut him off. He knew he had a little in a trust his father had left him, but it wouldn't be enough to pay for the house and all the help. And while Drew didn't care if he had to downsize, he didn't want to put his employees out of a job. If he just did this, this one favor, then he wouldn't have to worry. He could keep his share of the money and his employees. Everyone won. He wished he felt better about it.

"All right, Mother. Just let me text her to let her know what's going on."

"Oh, don't worry about it, dear. She's already with Avery probably relaxing in some tub full of mud. Call her afterward and you can share stories. Besides, the benefit starts in half an hour, so we need to get going."

Her words rubbed Drew wrong. Why wouldn't she want him to text Gwen? He glanced at his watch. It was five thirty. He was supposed to be picking up Gwen at six. Even if she was away from her phone, he wanted his text to be there. Gwen had shared too much about men lying and letting her down. He didn't want to be one of those men.

Wrangled into doing a benefit with my mother tonight. I'll fill you in later. Sorry, I must cancel.

"See, that took no time at all," Drew said with a triumphant smile at his mother. Now, even if she had some sinister plot planned, Gwen would know he'd had nothing to do with it.

"Very well. Shall we go?" His mother strode out of the room and Drew followed though he felt a little like a lamb being led to a slaughter.

"*A*very, what are you doing here?" Gwen asked as she opened the door. She had been expecting Drew even though he'd said he wasn't picking her up for another hour.

"Drew got called into a late meeting tonight. He sent me over and asked if I could entertain you for a bit until he was free. I thought maybe we could do a makeover and then go to dinner." She held up a bag that Gwen assumed contained hair and makeup items.

"Um, all right, sure." It wasn't that she and Avery never spoke, but this would be their first time hanging out as friends though Gwen wasn't sure she would call Avery a friend. She was nice to talk to, and she'd been very helpful whenever Gwen had questions about the donations, but that was about the extent of their relationship.

"Wonderful." Avery stepped into Gwen's living room and scanned the area. "Your place is lovely."

"Uh, thank you." It was nothing grand, but Gwen had decorated the place as nicely as she could. She'd been fortunate enough to find matching furniture for sale on Craig's list shortly after she moved in, and her decorations came from Ross.

"Let's sit at your dining room table. The light there looks good." Without waiting for an answer, Avery crossed the room and began removing things from the bag. A straightener, a curling iron, hair spray, gel, makeup.

Gwen shook her head, afraid of what she was getting

herself into, but she followed Avery and sat down in the chair she had pulled out.

"So, how are things going with Drew?" Avery asked as she picked up a brush and began running it through Gwen's hair. "It seems like you two are pretty happy."

"We are," Gwen said. In fact, things had been great with Drew lately. They had spent Thanksgiving just the two of them as Gwen didn't have family and Jacqueline hadn't invited either of them to dine with her. Drew didn't seem too upset his mother was giving him the silent treatment though it weighed on Gwen. She couldn't help feeling responsible for ruining their relationship.

"Except?" Avery asked.

Gwen bit her lip. She wasn't sure she trusted Avery, but she did need to talk to someone. "I just feel awful for driving a wedge between Drew and his mother. I've been praying every day they'll talk to each other, but-"

"Praying? You're a believer?" Avery set the brush down and sprayed Gwen's hair with some fruity smelling mist.

"Yes." Why did Gwen have the feeling Avery would use that against her?

"And Drew knows this?"

"Yes, he's been attending church with me." Unfortunately, he still hadn't given his life to God. It was the one thing keeping Gwen from giving him her whole heart. She wanted to be with a believer, and though she thought he was close, she'd assumed the same thing about Adam.

"Wow, that is surprising. I figured he would have turned his back on all that after Sarah."

Gwen blinked. "Sarah? Who's Sarah?"

"Sarah was a girl he was seeing when we met. She was the religious kind always dragging him to church. They were going to get married, but then she left to go do mission work. Broke his heart." Avery picked up the curling iron and twisted Gwen's hair around the metal rod.

"He never mentioned a Sarah." Nor had he mentioned attending church. He'd told her he was a holiday Christian. So, who wasn't telling the truth? Her gut told her not to trust Avery, but her insecurities and her past had her questioning Drew as well.

"I'm not surprised. He was rather embarrassed by the incident. He'd bought the ring and everything. He loved Sarah and decided he'd never date a believer after that, so I'm surprised you got him to a church again is all."

"Hmm." Gwen didn't know what else to say. She wanted to talk to Drew about this and get his side of the story. Avery had known him longer, but her story just didn't ring true for Gwen.

"But maybe he's over it now. He looks at you much the same way he used to look at Sarah." Avery finished with the curling iron and moved to applying makeup on Gwen. "Wow, you have great skin. I'm not going to do much, just a little shadow, some liner, and a hint of blush."

This was not much? Gwen felt as if her face had at least three extra layers on as Avery moved from one area to the next.

"I think I'm done. Why don't you go change into something a little dressier and I'll pack up?"

"Sure." Gwen headed to her room, hoping her face didn't look as awful as it felt. She made a beeline for the bathroom and flicked on the light. It was more makeup than she normally wore, but Avery had applied it tastefully. Gwen supposed she could leave it on for the evening.

She turned to her closet and flipped hangers until she landed on a simple black dress. With a long necklace, she would look...well, not elegant, but not dowdy either. Gwen slipped the dress on and grabbed an appropriate necklace from her jewelry box before heading back to the dining room.

"Perfect," Avery said. "I packed your bag for you to save time. We have reservations for dinner at six."

Gwen found that pushy but said nothing. Maybe Avery was just like that. She took the bag and motioned for Avery to lead the way, so she could lock the door behind her.

"Oh, do you mind if we take your car? I gave my driver the night off knowing you prefer to drive yourself."

"Uh sure." Had she told Avery she had an aversion to being driven? She thought back over their conversations but couldn't recall. Maybe Drew had mentioned it. It wasn't a big deal; it just unnerved her a little that Avery knew. As she unlocked the car door, she pushed the thought from her mind. She was determined to have a good time tonight and get to know Avery better.

CHAPTER 18

Drew tugged at his neckline as he followed his mother into the ballroom. She had insisted he wear a tie and brandished one from her purse when he explained he didn't have one with him. He hated ties. They felt like a noose, and this one even more so as it represented the leash his mother held on him. He would be so glad when this night was over, and he didn't have to attend any more of these events.

He still wasn't sure what he planned to do after, but he had enough money that he could take a few months to decide. A part of him wanted to return to the teaching degree he had never finished. Another part of him was considering something to help foster kids. Gwen was rubbing off on him. In fact, he'd been planning to tell her tonight that he had made the leap of faith and accepted Jesus as his savior, but he didn't want to do it over a text.

"Ah, here's our table," his mother said as she stopped in front of a table near the back.

"*This* is your table?" His mother hated sitting near the back. She felt her place was front and center and everyone should know it.

"Ah, well, it was a last-minute thing. I didn't think you would attend, and then when I decided on the offer to extend to you, the front tables were all full."

"Uh huh." Drew wasn't sure he was buying what his mother was selling. She was too chipper, and her eyes darted around the room as if she were looking for something or someone.

"Shall we sit?" She pulled out her chair and perched on the edge. Drew followed suit and sat beside her.

"I wonder if we know our other table guests." She leaned to her right. "I have an Emily S. here. How about you?"

Drew didn't care who was sitting to his left, but he leaned over to oblige his mother. "An Alexandra K." He rolled his eyes, certain he would be surrounded by women. Had this been an attempt by his mother to set him up with some rich woman so he'd forget Gwen? Well, it would not work.

"Oh, I think I know Alexandra K. Her mother used to attend my gardening club. She's a lovely thing. Just about your age. Blond and beautiful."

"Mother, I'm seeing Gwen, remember? Have been for over a month."

His mother puffed up like a peacock. "Well, that doesn't mean you can't be nice to the girl. I wonder if her mother will attend as well. Oh, there she is. Katarina, over here."

His mother waved her arm back and forth and hollered again to a woman across the room.

The woman, a stunning older blonde, smiled as she saw his mother's hand and headed their direction. Behind her trailed a younger version of herself. Blonde and beautiful was an understatement. Her daughter was easily one of the most striking women Drew had ever laid eyes on. *Is this a test Lord?* He prayed silently. *If it is, please don't let me fail.*

"Jacqueline, it is so good to see you again." Beside him, his mother stood to greet the woman who had a thick Russian accent. "You remember my daughter, Alexandra."

"Yes, of course, how nice to see you again. This is my son, Drew. I believe he was off at boarding school when you attended garden club, so I'm not sure you ever met."

Katarina's eyes shifted to Drew, who had stood when his mother had and now felt awkward and like a piece of meat at a market next to her. If this wasn't a set up, he would be surprised.

"I must say, Drew, that you are a very handsome young man, but then look at your mother. The apple does not fall far from the tree, no?"

Drew smiled politely and discreetly checked his watch. Ten more minutes. Just ten more minutes of small talk and the benefit would start. He could survive ten minutes.

"Alexandra, don't you think Drew has the most amazing eyes?" Katarina continued.

Alexandra stepped forward and looked at Drew. Her perfectly plucked brow arched just the tiniest bit before the corners of her lips pulled into a smile. Drew forced himself to stare into her eyes because he could see in his peripheral vision that she had a brilliant smile. One that could suck men in and ensnare them, and he didn't want to be a victim.

"They are a beautiful shade of blue," she said, her words lilting softly with her accent.

"Thank you," Drew said. "Yours are stunning as well, but might I suggest we all sit down? I'm sure our other table mates will arrive shortly."

As if summoned, a waitress came by and snatched the two remaining names off the table. "Sorry, they were unable to make it," she said before walking away.

"Well, that will give us more time to catch up and get to know one another," his mother said as they took their seats around the table.

Drew stifled a sigh as he folded his napkin in his lap. That was the last thing he wanted.

"Oh, dear," Alexandra said. "I think I have lost an earring. Drew, will you help me look? It must be on the ground."

Drew had no desire to crawl around on the ground for this woman he barely knew, but it would have been rude for him to decline. He scooted his chair back and dropped to his knees, scanning the area.

◈

"I don't understand," Gwen said as they entered the expensive hotel. "What are we doing here? I thought we had dinner reservations."

"We do, but I couldn't find my card in the car and I believe I dropped it here when I was working earlier. We'll just take a quick look in the ballroom and be on our way."

"All right." Gwen followed Avery down the elaborate hallway. As Avery pulled open the ballroom doors though, her heart stopped. She blinked, not believing her eyes. Drew was on his knees in front of some beautiful woman and holding something out to her. Was he proposing?

"What's the matter?" Avery asked. She followed Gwen's gaze and exhaled. "Oh dear. That's Sarah. She must have come back. I guess he's not over her after all."

Hot tears exploded in Gwen's vision, and she didn't wait to see more. With an anguished cry, she ran from the room. Her low heels pounded against the floor as she raced for the entry. This could not be happening. Not again. She'd told him about Adam. Why in the world would he do the same thing to her? Maybe he had never been into her. Maybe him taking her out had been part of some sick joke to poke fun at the poor, lower class.

She pushed the door of the hotel open and raced into the cold. Tiny white flakes pelted her in the face and chilled her tear-stained cheeks, but she didn't care. She just had to get away. As far away as she could from this place, from Drew. How could she have been so stupid?

Her keys nearly fell from her grip as she pulled them from her pocket with cold fingers. The temperature was dropping quickly. She needed to get home before the worst of the storm hit. There she could curl up with Tabby, flannel pajamas, and a big bowl of ice cream and drown her sorrows.

She shoved the key into the ignition, wiped her eyes, and started the car. The snow fell harder now, exploding against her windshield in tiny white balls. Gwen turned the wipers up as she pulled out of the parking lot. All she wanted to do was get home, but the snow and her tears were forcing her to drive slower than normal.

"Come on." She pounded the wheel in frustration as a car in front of her slowed to a near stop. She tapped her brakes, so as not to plow into the back of him and took the opportunity to wipe her eyes again. Her tears were falling freely now, racing each other down her cheeks.

The car ahead of her turned off, and Gwen pressed the accelerator. It had been wet enough earlier that she knew the streets would freeze soon and she wanted to be safely home before that happened.

She turned her wipers up another notch. The snow was coming in thick sheets now, obscuring the road almost completely. Gwen let her foot off the accelerator to slow her speed. Her turn was coming up somewhere, but she couldn't see the sign. Suddenly, something ran across the road. Gwen slammed on her brakes out of instinct and they locked up, sending the car into a spin. She yanked the wheel to the left and then to the right, but nothing helped.

The car veered to the left and Gwen sucked in her breath. She was on House hill - a street named for its extreme descent. As her car picked up speed, Gwen sent a prayer heavenward. *Please, Lord, don't let this be the end.*

CHAPTER 19

"*T*hank you, Drew, you are such a gentleman," Alexandra exclaimed as he handed the earring to her.

"No problem." As he stood, he caught sight of a familiar face in the doorway. Avery? What was she doing here? And why did she look so smug? "Excuse me, I'll be right back." He strode over to her. "What are you doing here, Avery?"

"Just delivering on a promise to your mother."

"My mother? What are you talking about?"

"That was lovely by the way. It looked just like a proposal. I couldn't have timed it better had I tried."

"Avery, are you okay?"

"It's so nice to see you've forgiven Sarah and you two are getting back together."

"Sarah?" Drew looked back at his table. "The woman's name is Alexandra and we're not together. I only met her tonight. She dropped her earring and I was giving it back to her."

A wicked smile flitted across Avery's features. "Yes, but that's not how Gwen saw it."

Drew's eyes widened. "Gwen was here? Where is she?"

Avery shrugged. "Gone. I doubt she'll be back. See, I told her all about Sarah, your ex-fiancée, who left to go do mission work, but it looks like she's back and you still have feelings for her."

White hot anger flared within Drew, and he clenched his fists to his side to keep from choking the woman in front of him. "What did you do?"

"What I had to do," she snapped at him. "I came back hoping we could pick up where we left off, but you had some gold digger on your mind."

"Avery, we would never have worked anyway. You said so yourself. Neither of us enjoy these snooty events..." he trailed off as realization dawned on him. "Except you do, but then why would you need me?" He exhaled and crossed his arms. "You need my money."

Avery's lips pulled into an unattractive sneer. "I lost mine in Europe and when I came home, I found that my father had gambled all of our family money away. I figured I could charm you again, we could marry, and then I'd take what was mine and keep painting, but there was Gwen. Sweet, little, innocent Gwen whom you needed to save." She rolled her eyes. "I figured she'd be easy to get rid of, but my note and flowers evidently didn't work, so I had to try something else."

Drew's head was spinning. How had he been so wrong about Avery? Had she always been this way or had her greed consumed her after she'd left?

"I went to your mother. She wanted Gwen out of your life as much as I did, and she paid me handsomely to get rid of her. Not as much as I would have gotten if I'd married you, but enough that I can probably invest it and rebuild."

"My mother paid you?" He glanced to his mother who stared back at them. At least she had the decency to look chagrined.

"She did, and this little setup," she waved her hand toward the ballroom, "was her idea. She took care of the invitation and your beautiful blond friend over there. I took care of Gwen. Made sure she was here to see what she needed to see to think you were a lying cheat."

Drew had never hit a woman, and he didn't want to start now, but it took all his energy to keep from ripping her to pieces. Instead, he lowered his voice and leaned in as if he were going to whisper in her ear. "I'm going to find Gwen. If you ever show your face around her again, I'll make sure your reputation is ruined forever. Do you understand me?"

She kept a brave face, but he saw a flicker of fear dance in her eyes. "Now, take your money and get out of my sight, Judas."

Avery stared at him a moment longer. Her eyes shifted to his mother and back to him. She opened her mouth to speak but then must have thought better of it. With a final angry stare, she spun on her heel and disappeared down the hallway.

Drew took a deep breath to calm his nerves before turning to his mother. His heart beat an insane rhythm in his chest, and he forced his feet to walk slowly and deliberately to give it time to slow down. "How could you, Mother?"

"I don't know what you're talking about," she said, tilting her nose up in the air.

"Avery told me everything. You paid her? Why? What's so horrible about Gwen that you had to pay someone to get her out of my life?"

"She's poor," his mother spat at him. "You are a Devonshire. You deserve more than some poor school teacher and keeping poor company would ruin our image."

Drew narrowed his eyes at his mother. "Well, you won't have to worry about our image any longer, Mother."

"There, see? I knew you would see it my way if you had a chance."

"You won't have to worry about our image because I will destroy it. I'm going to make sure everyone in this town knows what you did to Gwen."

"But, but, you can't," his mother stuttered. "We'll lose everything."

"We'll lose some things," he said. "You might have to downsize, but I'll keep what really matters. Honesty and integrity. The rest are just idols, and if you haven't figured it out by now, I no longer care about idols." With that, he turned and walked out of the room, leaving his mother and the other two women at his table gaping at him.

He pulled his phone from his pocket and dialed Gwen's number. It rang four times before her voicemail picked it up.

"Gwen? It's Drew. I know what you think you saw tonight, but it was staged. Please let me explain. I'm coming over to talk."

He ended that call and dialed another number. "Manuel, get the car ready," he said as he hit the hallway. He had a woman he needed to find and offer an apology.

CHAPTER 20

"Can't we go any faster, Manuel?" Drew was sitting beside him in the driver's seat instead of in his usual seat in the back.

"I'm sorry, sir. The snow is bad. I'm going as fast as I can." Manuel's hands gripped the steering wheel tightly in a perfect three and nine formation.

"I know, I don't mean to pressure you. I'm just worried about her." He closed his eyes and leaned his head back against the rest, sending a prayer up to his newfound savior. *Lord, help me find her. I can't lose her like this.*

"Mr. Devonshire, we are here, sir." Manuel was shaking his arm. Drew opened his eyes. Had he fallen asleep?

"Do you see her car?"

"No, but it is hard to see anything. The snow is getting worse. The news station said it is near blizzard conditions and that we should stay off the streets."

"All right, Manuel, let me see if she's in there. I'll be quick if I must, but I have to explain."

Manuel nodded, and Drew pulled the door open. A wall of white greeted him, and the snow whipped and tugged at his coat. He shut the door behind him and carefully made his way up the walk to Gwen's apartment. "Gwen?" He pounded on the door. "Gwen, if you're there, please let me in."

Behind him, the door of the apartment across the way opened. "Yo, man, I don't think she's there. She left like an hour ago and ain't been back since."

"Thank you," Drew said. If Gwen wasn't in her apartment where would she have gone? Carrie. Drew hurried back to the limo and pulled out his cell phone when he was back in the warmth. He hadn't thought he would ever call her, but he was glad he had gotten her number.

"Hello?"

"Carrie? It's Drew. Is Gwen there?"

"No, I thought she was with you. Didn't the two of you have a date?"

"We did, but there was a miscommunication. If she calls you, will you let me know?"

"Of course. Should I be worried, Drew?" He could tell by the sound of her voice that she already was worried.

"I don't know yet, Carrie, but pray. I'll call you if I find anything out."

He hung up the phone and stared at it. Now what did he do?

"Sir?"

"Hang on, Manuel, I'm thinking." Drew closed his eyes again. He needed help of the omniscient kind. His lips moved slightly as he prayed for wisdom and guidance to find Gwen. Then his eyes snapped open. "Go back."

"Back where, sir? To the hotel?"

"Yes, like you're going back to the hotel, but we won't go that far. Just go slowly."

Manuel nodded and eased the limo out of the parking lot. They started back the way they had come with Drew hollering out a turn now and then. "Right here." "Left at the next street." Drew had no idea where they were going, but he could feel the words in his bones.

Suddenly, he sat up straighter and pointed. "There." Ahead of them, they could just make out the flicker of something in the snow. Drew noticed the darkened houses on either side of the road. Someone had hit a power line, and he knew, he just knew it was Gwen.

Sure enough, a few minutes later, her car came into sight. The car was pinned underneath the fallen power pole. "Call 911," he said to Manuel before sprinting out of the car toward Gwen.

A live wire flashed and jumped on the street and Drew gave it a wide berth. He was relieved to see the pole had missed Gwen when he reached the car, but they would still need the jaws of life to get her out. The pole had crushed the passenger side around her and mushed the dash, so it was pinning her thighs.

He yanked on her door, but it was no use. Her window was a spiderweb of cracks, so Drew jammed his elbow into the upper right corner. The glass shattered inward, falling on Gwen like iridescent drops. He hoped none of them would cut her, but he needed to know she was still alive.

"Gwen?" He reached in and felt for a pulse. There, but just barely. "Gwen? Can you hear me? Help is on the way, okay? Stay with me. Help is on the way."

Her eyes opened the tiniest bit. "Drew, what are you doing here?"

"Shh." He patted her hair. "Don't talk. I came to apologize. What you saw wasn't truth. It was staged to make you run."

"How did you find me?"

Drew shook his head. "I don't know. I followed a feeling."

The corners of her lips twitched as if she were trying to smile. "I think that might have been God talking to you, Drew. Now do you believe he exists?"

Drew chuckled. "I do, Gwen. I accepted him earlier today. I was going to tell you tonight."

"That's good," she said and then her eyes closed again.

"Gwen?" He didn't want to shake her. He had no idea if she'd injured her neck. "Stay with me, Gwen."

The blessed sound of sirens reached his ears, but they could not come fast enough for Drew.

CHAPTER 21

"*H*ow is she?" Carrie cried as she rushed toward Drew. Knowing she would be worried, he had called her as soon as the ambulance took Gwen away.

He shook his head. "I don't know yet. The doctor hasn't said."

"What was she doing driving in the snow? Didn't she know the storm was hitting tonight?"

"I don't think anyone knew it would hit that quickly," Drew said, avoiding her original question. He didn't want to tell her Gwen had been trying to get away from him even if what she had seen had been a lie.

"Mr. Devonshire?" Drew and Carrie both turned to the approaching doctor.

"Yes, I'm Drew Devonshire. Is… is she all right?"

"Physically, yes. She was very lucky the pole missed her. She'll have some bruising on her chest and legs from the impact, but that's not our main concern. Does Gwen have family we should notify?"

"Gwen's parents are dead," Carrie said in a small voice, "and she hasn't seen her foster parents in years. We're her family."

The doctor looked from Carrie to Drew. "Well, our bigger concern is that she isn't waking up. It could be that her body is just in shock, and she'll come out of it soon, but we don't know for sure."

Carrie sobbed and buried her face in Drew's chest. Instinctually, his arm wrapped around her shoulders. "Thank you, doctor. Please keep us informed if anything changes."

"I will." The doctor nodded before turning and walking back down the hallway.

"Drew, what are we going to do? I can't lose my best friend." Carrie's voice was muffled as she cried into his chest.

He led her to the seating area and pulled her down next to him. He took her hands in his and squeezed them. "Carrie, I don't believe God brought Gwen and I together only to have this end in tragedy. She has had too much sorrow in her life, and she deserves some happiness."

Carrie sniffed. "Yes, she does."

"So, we pray, and we sit with her. Why don't I take the first shift? You should go and check on Tabby, especially since Gwen might be here for a few days."

Carrie nodded and wiped her cheeks. "Right. I can do that, and I'll close the shop tomorrow, so I can sit with Gwen."

"That sounds like a good plan." Drew stood and pulled her up beside him. "Drive home safely please."

"I will, but Drew, you better call me if she wakes up."

"I promise," Drew said. He watched Carrie exit the hospital into the blinding snow before collapsing back into the chair. He did believe God had plans for them, but it sure was hard to trust that right now.

"Drew Devonshire, I want a word with you."

His head popped up at his mother's voice. What was she doing here? How had she known where he was? Knowing his mother, she had pinged his cell phone. He certainly wouldn't put it past her. "Mother, what are you doing here? Haven't you done enough?"

"Done enough?" she asked. "What exactly have I done besides look out for you?"

He glared at her. "Do you not know, Mother? Gwen was in an accident after she fled the hotel. She's in a coma now, so I hope you're happy."

His mother reeled back as if punched in the stomach. "She's... but she's going to wake up, right?"

"They don't know, Mother. They have no idea if she'll wake up again. Do you know the life this woman has had? No, you don't because you never bothered to get to know her. She lost her parents when she was twelve. She had a foster father who locked her in a closet. The one man she let get close to her proposed and then she found out he was cheating on her, and still this woman wears a smile. She became a teacher to help children like herself. She donates time and money to local foster care charities. She may not be wealthy monetarily, but she is rich in so many other ways, Mother, and you could never be bothered to see that."

His mother's hand covered her mouth and she sank down in a chair. For a moment she sat there, as if letting the words sink in. "Drew, I am so sorry. You're right. I judged her without knowing her, and I can see now how very wrong I was." She looked up at him with tear-filled eyes. "Please, tell me that you'll forgive me."

Drew wanted to snap at her, to tell her that he would never forgive her, especially if something happened to Gwen, but the sermons the pastor had been preaching on forgiveness resounded in his mind. He knew he had to forgive his mother. It was what God said, and it was right, but it wasn't easy. "I'm trying to, Mother. With the help of God, I'm trying to, but when Gwen wakes up, you will apologize to her as well. And if, after that, you don't want to be around her, that's your choice. But I am choosing Gwen, and you will either accept this relationship or we will part ways."

She wiped a tear from the corner of her eye. Drew couldn't remember the last time he had seen her cry, but he wasn't going to let that affect his decision. "I will, Drew. I haven't been the best example, but I'm going to change, and I will make this up to both you and Gwen." She stood and pulled her shoulders back. "I promise."

Drew hoped his mother would make good on that promise, but he didn't care right now. Right now, he just wanted to see Gwen, to hold her hand, and to pray.

CHAPTER 22

*G*wen tried to open her eyes, but they felt glued shut. And her body ached everywhere. What had happened?

"Hey, don't move too much."

Was that Drew's voice? Drew. Suddenly, the memories came flooding back. Drew proposing to his ex, her running out, and the car spinning out of control. She must have crashed.

It took all her energy, but she forced her eyelids open. The room was hazy, and she found it hard to focus. Then a face appeared in her vision. "Drew, what are you doing here?" Her voice came out soft and raspy. How long had it been since she had spoken out loud?

His face was still mostly a blur, but she could make out his smile. "Are you kidding? I'm never leaving your side again."

"But Sarah-"

He shook his head. "Sarah was never real. Avery made her up to scare you away. She also sent the flowers and the note."

"Why?"

"She needed you out of the way, so she could try to entice me to marry her. She wanted my money. Evidently, she lost all of hers when she went to Europe. We had dated briefly before she left, and I guess she thought we could pick up where we left off. I don't know what happened to her while she was gone, but she is certainly not the same woman she was when she left."

Gwen let all of this sink in. She had left the hotel thinking that yet another man had betrayed her when it was really him who had been betrayed. Still that didn't explain why he was at the hotel to begin with. "Avery said you were working late. Why were you at the hotel?"

Drew's face fell. "I'm afraid my mother was in on some of this scheme too. She didn't want me falling for a girl with no money, so she hired Avery to get rid of you. She came to me the night of the benefit and told me I could keep my half of the fortune if I attended one final benefit. I was trying to save the jobs of my employees, so I went." He grabbed her hand. "I called you though and left a message. Did you never get it?"

Gwen shook her head slightly. Pain still pounded in her head like an orchestra of hammers. "No, but Avery came over that night and did a makeover on me. I was in my room for a few minutes. She could have done something to my phone. Then she packed my bag. I thought that was odd at the time, but I never bothered to check it. Was my bag in the car?"

Drew's eyes dropped to the floor for a moment. "Gwen, a power pole hit the car. It barely missed you. Shortly after they got you out, a spark from a downed line touched the gas that must have been leaking and the car went up in flames. They couldn't get anything else out. I'm sorry."

Gwen closed her eyes. She didn't care about the car. Not really. It was old - a 1993 Mitsubishi Mirage - but it had been paid for, and she couldn't afford to take out a loan on a new one, especially as she was missing work. Work. Her eyes popped open. "Drew, how long have I been here?"

Another side glance and his hand raked across his stubbled chin. Two sure signs it was longer than she hoped. "A week. You hit your head pretty hard and were in a coma."

"A week?" The words came out barely more than a squeak. "Do I even still have a job?"

"Of course, you do. I went there myself and explained the situation. That Carol in your office is a big fan of yours."

Gwen managed a small chuckle. "She's just glad she finally knows who the flowers were from."

At that, Drew let out a deep laugh. The chocolate tones of it tickled Gwen's ears. She could get used to that laugh. "I feel like you told me, Drew, but how did they find me? It sounds like it was close."

Two lines of concern creased Drew's brow. "You don't remember?"

"Guess not."

"I found you, Gwen. You spoke to me in the car. I thought you'd remember."

"Wait, you found me? How?"

Drew's smile widened, and a light danced behind his eyes. "I think God told me. I accepted him that morning and was going to tell you that night. When I found out what my mother and Avery had done, I had Manuel drive me to your place, but you weren't there. I called Carrie, but she didn't know where you were either, so I prayed. On the way back to the hotel, I heard- no, I felt directions in my head. Those directions led us straight to you."

"That's amazing, Drew." Gwen had thought he seemed different. Lighter, more smiley. This news explained it. "Tabby. Did someone take care of Tabby?"

"Don't worry. Carrie's been cat sitting dutifully. Now, if you feel up to it, you have another visitor."

Gwen wasn't sure she felt like more visitors. She still didn't know the extent of her injuries, but he seemed so excited that she couldn't say no.

"Promise you'll hear her out," Drew said as he headed for the hallway.

Gwen didn't like the sound of that. Surely, he hadn't brought Avery here. She knew the Bible preached forgiveness, but she was going to need a little time. But it wasn't Avery who walked in. It was Jacqueline, and contrite didn't begin to describe her appearance. The haughty expression was gone from her face, replaced with what appeared to be genuine concern.

"Hello, Gwen."

"Jacqueline." She better have something good to say because as far as Gwen was concerned, she wasn't much better than Avery. Who hired someone to get rid of their son's girlfriend?

"I'm glad you agreed to see me."

"Well, in all fairness, I didn't know it was you." Stop it. Ephesians 4:32 filled her mind, and Gwen knew she needed to forgive Jacqueline as God had forgiven her.

"Yes, I suppose that's true. I came here today for a few reasons. The first is to tell you how truly sorry I am. Money and my place in society had become my idol. Drew's been helping me see the error of those ways." She flashed a tight smile Drew's direction. "I should never have tried to separate you. He cares for you a great deal."

She paused as if waiting for an acceptance of her apology, so Gwen gave what she could. "Thank you, Jacqueline. That means a lot."

The woman twisted her hands together in a nervous gesture and then reached into her bag. She withdrew a small green box with a bright red bow. "I know Christmas is still a few days away, but I wanted to give this to you now. I hope you'll accept it."

Gwen took the present. Curiosity outweighed her dislike of the woman, and she opened the lid. Inside was a key. She looked up to Jacqueline. "I don't understand."

"Drew told me the accident totaled your car, and I feel responsible for you crashing that night. I've already taken care of all your hospital bills, but I knew you'd need new transportation. This is a key to your new car. I wasn't sure what you would like, but Drew mentioned something about a Mini Cooper."

Gwen smiled as she touched the key. That conversation had happened over lunch one day. They had ventured into a topic of their love for all things British, and Gwen had told him of her secret desire to own a Mini Cooper one day.

"If you don't like it, I can have it returned, but-"

"I'm sure I'll love it, Jacqueline."

"Oh, good." Her hands twisted together again. "I have one more thing then. I'd like you to spend Christmas with us. I know I messed up Thanksgiving, but Drew and I have bonded over the last week, and I'd like to make it up to you."

Gwen nodded, her heart warming. If Jacqueline was acting, she was putting on quite the show. Gwen was much more inclined to believe the woman was changing or trying to at least. "I would like that."

Jacqueline's eyes brightened and the somber expression on her face lifted. "Yes? Oh, that's wonderful. Thank you, Gwen. I believe you might be as amazing as Drew claims you are."

"All right, Mother," Drew said, "I think you've propped me up enough. Don't put me too high on that pedestal or I might fall off."

"He's a keeper," Jacqueline whispered to Gwen before patting her arm. "It's time I let you rest anyway. I've got a Christmas party to plan." She flashed a small wave and then walked out of the room.

"I missed a lot in a week," Gwen said with a smile. She

felt a little like Alice in Wonderland. Everything seemed different.

Drew issued another one of those deep laughs. "You did. God works in mysterious ways, and though I wouldn't wish your accident on anyone, I'm thankful it made my mother see the error of her ways. Oh, and I checked with the doctor. He will come examine you, but as long as he finds nothing out of the ordinary, he said you could go home today."

Home. She could think of no place she'd rather be.

CHAPTER 23

"You look beautiful," Carrie said as she batted Gwen's hand down. "Stop messing with it."

"I'm sorry. It itches." Gwen had agreed to let Carrie take her for a full day of pampering before the Christmas dinner party. Her hands and feet were neatly painted, her skin was scrubbed fresh, and her hair was pulled up, but the woman had put a few too many pins in her hair and they were digging into Gwen's scalp. She tried one more time to scratch, but Carrie shot her a disapproving look. "Okay, fine. Thank you for coming with me by the way."

"Are you kidding? My pleasure. I want to live in a place like this someday. Who would have thought that you would live in a mansion before I did?"

Gwen scoffed and ducked her head as they walked up the ornate path. "I'm not living in one yet."

"You will be. I've seen the way Drew looks at you. He

may not propose tonight, but if I were a betting woman, I'd wager he pops the question within six months, and you're married before next Christmas." Carrie pressed the doorbell.

Gwen hoped Carrie was right. Ever since she had returned from the hospital, her apartment had seemed lonelier. And even when Drew came over to bring her food or do a devotional with her, the stillness only abated while he was there. As soon as he left, it creeped in again with a quiet ferocity. Gwen knew it was because she had finally found the man she was supposed to be with. She could feel it in her soul every time they were together.

The door opened, and Pierre smiled at them. "Good evening, Miss Gwen and friend. Please come inside and join the festivities." He stepped back to allow them entrance, and Gwen gasped.

The room had been transformed into a magical wonderland. Christmas lights hung from the ceilings, tinsel draped across every surface, and at least three trees sat around the room.

"It's beautiful," she said in a hushed voice.

"Not nearly as beautiful as you." Drew had come up behind her and his arm circled her waist. His voice was quiet in her ear. He spun her around and stared into her eyes. "I'm afraid, Miss Gwen, that you are standing under mistletoe and that I am forced to supply you with a kiss."

Gwen giggled and glanced up to see Drew holding a sprig over their heads. "Well, we don't want to mess with tradition, now do we?"

"We do not," he said as his lips found hers.

Now this was home. In Drew's arms, in a warm house, with Christmas music playing in the background. This was the relationship Gwen had hoped for.

"All right, you two love birds," Carrie said breaking into the kiss. "You can resume that later. I, for one, would love some eggnog."

With a smile, Drew laced his fingers through Gwen's and led her into the kitchen. Jacqueline stood at the island icing cookies.

"Oh good, you made it. I just finished this batch. What do you think?" She turned the plate around and Gwen bit her lip to keep from smiling. The santas looked more like clouds and the colors on the trees clumped together, but she knew Jacqueline had worked hard on them.

"They look beautiful, and I'm sure they taste just as good."

"They better," Ernesto said stepping into the kitchen. "I worked hard on them all day." His eyes fell to the iced disasters. "Oh, no, what have you done to my cookies?"

"Come on," Drew tugged on Gwen's hand. "I have something for you." He pulled her out of the kitchen and over to one of the trees where he picked up a small gift and handed it to her.

"It's not present time yet," she said.

"Think of it as a gift to enhance your outfit," he said with a smile.

Gwen glanced down at her outfit. It was a hunter green

dress with a red sash. She wasn't sure what else it needed, but she humored him and took the small package. As she lifted the lid, her lips parted, and emotion welled up in her throat. Inside was a dainty gold locket.

"Do you like it?"

"I love it," Gwen answered. She flicked the clasp and tears flooded her eyes. Somehow Drew had found a picture of her mother and father and they stared back at her now.

"This way you can always have them close to your heart." Drew picked the locket up and fastened it around her neck. Gwen stared at it one more time. She had never had a more thoughtful gift.

"Thank you, Drew Devonshire. This means the world to me."

His hands slid to her shoulders. "You mean the world to me, Gwen Rodgers. You've turned my world completely upside down in the short time that I've known you, but in a good way. You brought my mother and I closer together. You've pushed me to follow my dreams, and you've made me a better man. You are my Christmas miracle, and I love you."

"I love you too." Gwen wrapped her arms around his neck and let herself melt in his embrace. This would be a Christmas she would remember for a long time to come.

The End!

. . .

*I*f you want to follow Carrie's story, be sure to check out The Billionaire's Cowboy Groom.

*I*f you liked this story and would like to know when the next book will be out, then please join my newsletter. I'm offering a free sample of my next book Free Sample!

IT'S NOT QUITE THE END!

Thank you so much for reading *The Billionaire's Christmas Miracle*. The Billionaire's Christmas Miracle was a fun book to write. I loved the idea of Drew, a wealthy good guy looking for something real, and Gwen, being the down-to-earth teacher (not unlike myself).

It was fun to do a Cinderella take. Perhaps I'll dabble in some more fairy tales in the future, but before I could even do that, readers wanted Gwen's and Drew's wedding, so of course I had to do that and decided giving Carrie her own book would be the perfect way. Keep reading for a sneak peek.

I hope you enjoyed the story as well. If you did, would you do me a favor? If you did, please leave a review. It really helps. It doesn't have to be long - just a few words to help other readers know what they're getting.

I'd love to hear from you, not only about this story, but about the characters or stories you'd like read in the future. I'm always looking for new ideas and if I use one of your characters or stories, I'll send you a free ebook and paperback of the book with a special dedication. Write to me at loranahoopes@gmail.com. And if you'd like to see what's coming next, be sure to stop by authorloranahoopes.com

I also have a weekly newsletter that contains many wonderful things like pictures of my adorable children, chances to win awesome prizes, new releases and sales I might be holding, great books from other authors, and anything else that strikes my fancy and that I think you would enjoy. I'll even send you the first chapter of my newest (maybe not even released yet) book if you'd like to sign up.

Even better, I solemnly swear to only send out one newsletter a week (usually on Tuesday unless life gets in the way which with three kids it usually does). I will not spam you, sell your email address to solicitors or anyone else, or any of those other terrible things.

And if you're interested in meeting the rest of the billionaires in the series, be sure to check out The Billionaire's Cowboy Groom. Turn the page for a sneak peek.

Fallen in love with Drew and Gwen? I did too along with designer Carrie Bliss, so I figured she needed her own story. Of course, Carrie is complicated, so her story had to be too. Bet you won't be expecting this....

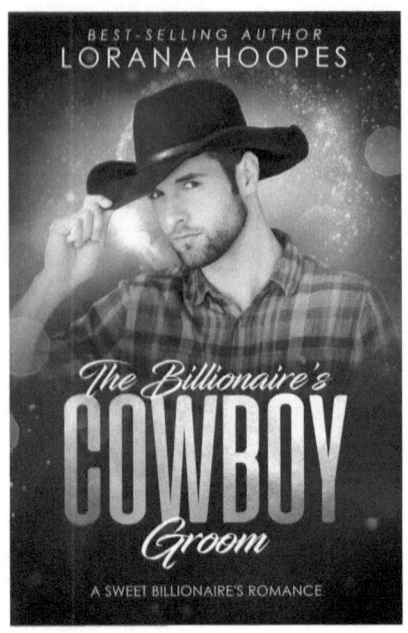

The Billionaire's Cowboy Groom

She's finally found the man she wants to marry...

There's just one problem. She married a man years ago in Vegas and never got divorced. Now, she must travel to Texas to get him to sign the papers.

He knew she was the one for him...

Though she disappeared after the wedding, Cal has never given up hope that she will come back into his life, but when she does, can he convince her to stay?

What if it was meant to be....

. . .

ead on for a taste of The Billionaire's Cowboy Groom....

THE BILLIONAIRE'S COWBOY GROOM
PREVIEW

*C*arrie zipped up the back of her best friend's dress and stepped back to admire it.

"Oh my goodness, Carrie, this is more beautiful than I even imagined." Gwen fingered the white satin, her hand trailing across the lace and bead detail. She turned and studied the image in the full-length mirror. With her red hair pulled up, her slender shoulders were even more defined in the strapless dress.

"Well, you deserve it. Besides, if you are going to marry Drew Devonshire and become a Devonshire, then you must dress like one." Carrie smiled at the vision that was Gwen. The white pearls and lace accentuated her creamy skin, and her green eyes sparkled. Happiness filled Carrie that she was able to make Gwen feel so good about herself.

"You are the best friend a girl could ask for." Gwen turned from the mirror and enveloped Carrie in a hug. "Now, let's get you dressed. Alyssa should be back soon."

Gwen had met Alyssa a few months after Drew proposed. Evidently, Drew had gone to college with Maxwell Banks, and they had reconnected when Drew searched for friends to make his groomsmen. It hadn't been too hard to find him considering they were both billionaires.

Max and Alyssa had visited, and Gwen and Alyssa had hit it off. They became close enough friends that Gwen had asked her to be a bridesmaid. Carrie didn't mind. Gwen needed more friends, and she liked Alyssa too. And of course, Peyton was a doll.

The door opened then and Alyssa and Peyton rushed in. Well, Peyton rushed in, Alyssa's entry was more of a waddle seeing as how she was eight and a half months pregnant. "Sorry, Gwen, when you gotta go, you gotta go."

"Wow, Miss Gwen, you look so pretty," Peyton stared up at Gwen with wide eyes. "Almost as pretty as Mommy looked when she married Daddy." Peyton looked back to Alyssa, her eyes full of admiration.

The girls all laughed. "Well, I wouldn't expect to look prettier than your mommy." Gwen smiled at Alyssa over Peyton's head. "And don't worry about the time. Your dress is here. Carrie was just about to get dressed as well."

"I realize it's not my wedding, but I feel like a chicken with its head cut off." Alyssa patted her pregnant belly. "How do you two keep up here?"

"I hire help." Carrie laughed as she slipped out of her clothes and into her bridesmaid dress. The emerald green satin hugged her figure like a second skin. She was glad she had been so strict with her diet lately, or the dress might not have fit her. "I've had to hire another designer to help me."

"It's because you are so amazing," Gwen said. "I mean this dress is stunning." She twirled in front of the mirror again.

"I'd say she's a fan." Alyssa chuckled as she stepped into her own emerald green dress. Gwen had chosen emerald green because she thought both Carrie and Alyssa would look good in it. Alyssa's hair was a dark brown unlike Carrie's red locks, but the emerald green was a color that brought out the best in both of them. "I wish I had known you when I got married. I would have loved to have worn a dress you designed."

Carrie stepped over to the mirror to check her reflection. "I saw your wedding picture. Your dress was beautiful."

"Did you see my dress at Mommy's wedding too?" Peyton asked. She was already in her flower girl dress and practicing throwing fake petals from her basket.

Carrie turned, smiled, and squatted down to the little girl's level. "As a matter of fact, I did. You looked just as pretty then as you do now." She tapped the end of the girl's nose earning a giggle in reply.

"Yes, it was beautiful," Alyssa said picking up the original thread of conversation again, "but there's something about having a friend make your dress that makes it extra special. I mean if you hadn't made this one, I doubt I would have found one that fit. I am as big as a house."

"You're welcome and you still look radiant," Carrie said. "When is the baby due?"

"A month. Can you believe that? It's a good thing you didn't plan this wedding any later, Gwen or they might not have let me fly."

"I'm sure Max would have found a way to get you here," Carrie said with a laugh. "I don't know him well, but he seems like a take charge kind of guy."

"Oh, he is that all right." Alyssa smoothed her dress and turned in front of the mirror. "What about you, Carrie? When are you going to marry that handsome French man I met? What was his name?"

"Philippe." Carrie shrugged her shoulders. "I'm not sure. He hasn't asked yet, but we've only been dating a few months." Of course, that was forever in Carrie's dating history. For as long as memory served her, she had flitted from one man to the next. Obviously, she was looking for something, but she wasn't sure what yet. She hoped she it would smack her in the face when she found it so she didn't miss it.

"Well, I'm sure it will be beautiful whenever it happens." Alyssa rubbed her belly again.

"And I'm sure this baby will be beautiful," Gwen said. "You better send pictures."

"Of course I will. Chances are he'll resemble this one though." She hugged Peyton to her. "Max's genes seem to run strong. Thank you, Gwen, for letting her be your flower girl."

"Yes, thank you, Miss Gwen. I promise to do a good job." Peyton's innocent face held the sincerest expression Carrie had ever seen on a person so young.

"I know you will, sweetie. Your mom said you are a natural at throwing flowers. And I have no younger sisters or nieces, so you are doing me the big favor." Gwen picked up the bag of flower petals and filled Peyton's basket.

Suddenly music carried into the room. "I think that might be our cue," Carrie said. "Everybody ready?"

"I can't believe it's finally time." Gwen's voice dripped with happiness and awe. Her face shone, and her smile stretched from one ear to the other.

As Carrie opened the door and led the way to the sanctuary, she wondered if she would ever have the same expression on her face. When would it be her turn?

*C*al Roper looked down into the basket of baked goods as he tried to come up with the right words. Though everything looked and probably was delicious, he needed to find some way to make Ginny understand he wasn't interested in her romantically. She was as sweet as cherry pie, but he preferred apple.

"Thanks, Ginny, this was real nice of you," Cal said as he looked back up at the perky blond.

"Oh, you know me, Cal, always baking more than I need." She dropped her eyes to the ground and her toe dug a circle in the soft dirt. "So, I thought to myself - who could use some homemade goodies? And you popped right into my head." She glanced up and flashed him a megawatt smile revealing nearly every one of her teeth as she batted her eyes at him.

Cal supposed she was waiting for more than a thank-you. An invitation to dinner maybe or a ride on the mares, but he couldn't do it. He wouldn't lead the poor girl on.

"Well, I do appreciate it, and I'm sure Stacy will as well, right, sis?" He flashed his sister a help-me-out-will-you glance as he spoke.

Stacy opened her mouth to reply, but Ginny beat her to it. "Not that I'm sure you're not a good cook, Stacy," she added as if just realizing how insulting her words might have sounded to his sister.

Stacy held up her hands. "I take no offense. Cal does his own cooking. I just work here, but I'm sure we both will enjoy these muffins. It was real sweet of you to think of Cal."

Ginny smiled again and turned her eyes back to Cal. Her smile faltered when she realized he wasn't going to extend any sort of invitation. "All right, well I better be getting my own dinner going, so I guess I'll see you both at church on Sunday."

"We'll be there," Cal said, "and thanks again." He lifted the basket and forced a small smile.

"She likes you," Stacy said as Ginny walked away.

Cal sighed and dropped the basket onto the porch. "I suspected." Ginny was a nice girl. Cute with a bubbly personality and a believer, but his heart belonged to someone else.

"But?" Stacy pressed.

Cal shrugged. "But I'm not interested."

"You haven't been interested in the last three women who have shown an interest in you. You didn't have enough in common with Gabriella, you had too much in common with Heather, and Sophie lived too far away."

"Well, she did," Cal said. "I don't want a long-distance relationship."

Stacy fixed her steely gray eyes on him. She might be a year younger than him, but she could turn a heart to ice with her fierce expression. He would want her watching his back in a fight any day. "Cal, it's been six years. When are you going to let that woman go?"

"When God tells me it's time." He took his Stetson off and wiped the light sheen of sweat from his forehead though he wasn't sure if the sweat was from his recently finished chores or this conversation. "I know you think I'm crazy, but I married her and that means something to me. God hasn't told me it's time to move on yet, so I'm going to follow His will until He does."

Stacy's eyes softened. "Cal, I understand you want to do God's will, but you married this woman on a whim in Vegas. That's not what God had planned when He created marriage."

Cal nodded. While Stacy didn't have the whole story, she was right that he shouldn't have married the woman. Cal hadn't even believed in love at first sight, but when he'd seen the fiery red head in the casino, his heart had jumped. It spun. It danced the tango in his chest, and he just knew he couldn't lose her. After spending hours talking with her, he'd proposed to her, and she'd said yes. An all-night wedding chapel had been delighted to take their money, and Cal had spent an amazing night with the woman. Unfortunately, she hadn't been quite as excited about the marriage the next morning. She had begged him for an annulment and when he'd refused, she had thrown her ring at him and left.

"I know you write her every year." Stacy continued breaking into his walk down memory lane. "Has she ever responded?"

"Not yet, but she will." Every year on their anniversary, Cal sent her a card requesting a rekindling of their relationship. Every year, he heard nothing from her - he honestly wasn't even sure if his letters were even getting to her. Still, Cal felt deep down in his bones that someday he would hear from her. He might not have waited on God's timing to marry her, but now that they were married, he was determined to wait on God's timing to make it right. And God kept telling him to wait. So, he would. He would wait as long as he had to.

*C*arrie linked arms with Scott as Alyssa and Max reached the front. She had hoped to be able to walk the aisle with Philippe, but Scott was Drew's best friend. It only made sense he would be the best man. Besides, she would have plenty of time with Philippe at the reception, and he would be sitting in the first few rows on Gwen's side. She would have a great view of him.

"Ready?" Scott asked.

"Absolutely." In step, they walked up the aisle parting ways at the stage. Carrie stepped to her left to stand beside Alyssa and Scott went to his right to stand between Max and Drew. Carrie turned to face the congregation as the music changed. Her eyes scanned for Philippe first who flashed her a charming smile. She returned it and then shifted her gaze to the back of the church to watch Gwen enter.

The lights hit the pearls and sequins on the dress as she entered, and Carrie smiled as gasps of delight echoed around the room. She had never been prouder of one of her designs.

Gwen handed her the bouquet as she stepped on the platform and took Drew's hands.

"Dearly beloved, we are gathered here today to celebrate the marriage of Gwen Rodgers and Drew Devonshire. On the outside, they may seem like opposites - a teacher and a billionaire - but they have learned one of the most important lessons in life. They have learned to see past money and outside appearance and into the heart. It's what's in the heart that matters most, and in that respect, they are two of a kind. They love each other, and they love the Lord."

Carrie glanced at Philippe as the minister spoke. "You look beautiful," Philippe mouthed to her, and a blush stole across her cheeks. Could he be the one for her? She hadn't seen any red flags that sent her running yet, but she had expected to feel something different if he was the one. Some tug on her heart, the sound of fireworks, something.

"Do you Drew, take this woman as your wife to have and

to hold through sickness and in health, forsaking all others until death do you part?"

Carrie shook her head to clear the thoughts. She had a job to do, and she needed to pay attention.

Drew's smile lit up his whole face as he said, "I do."

"And do you Gwen take this man as your husband to have and to hold through sickness and in health forsaking all others until death do you part?"

"I do."

"Then by the power vested to me by the great state of New York, I now pronounce you husband and wife. You may kiss the bride."

Carrie cheered along with the rest of the congregation as Drew leaned forward and kissed Gwen. Then they faced the church and held their hands up before running out the aisle. Carrie took Scott's arm and followed suit. They burst out the doors and joined Gwen and Drew in the foyer. Max, Alyssa, and Peyton joined them a moment later.

"Congratulations, Gwen," Carrie said enveloping her in another hug. "You looked so beautiful."

"I'll second that," Drew said. "Carrie, that dress is perfection."

"Well, I had a good model." She handed the bridal bouquet back to Gwen. "You might need these."

"I might, but I have a sneaking suspicion it'll be finding its way back to you soon enough." Gwen took the flowers and flashed a knowing glance at Carrie.

"I'm not sure about that," Carrie said with a shake of her head. "Philippe doesn't seem in any hurry to propose."

"He will," Alyssa said joining the conversation. "I predict a wedding in your near future."

Carrie appreciated the sentiments of her friends, but she wasn't so sure. Philippe may have been her longest relationship in years, but they were only going on four months. It was way too early for him to propose, and she was still sorting out her feelings. "Come on, we better get to the reception area before the stampede hits," Carrie said changing the subject.

"Just not too fast." Alyssa placed her hands on her large belly. "This pregnant woman can only go so quickly."

"We'll see you there in a minute," Gwen said as Drew pulled her toward the holding room where they would wait a few minutes to give the rest of the congregation time to get to the reception area.

Carrie led the way down the hallway and opened the doors to the reception area. It was decorated with white lights and tulle. White roses nestled in green foliage covered every tabletop and large windows granted expansive views of the city. The elegance, though understated, permeated the room. Gwen's personality shone through in every simple touch.

"Wow," Peyton said beside Carrie. "It looks like a princess lives here."

Carrie nodded. "Her wedding planner was pretty amazing, but I think most of this was Gwen's idea. I'm guessing that's our table up there on the stage. Shall we go find a seat?"

"Yes, please," Alyssa said. "I would love to get out of these shoes."

By the time they sat down, the rest of the guests were making their way in. Philippe joined Carrie at the head table. "That was a nice ceremony."

"It was." Carrie stared at him a moment wondering if he ever imagined what their wedding might look like.

"Ladies and gentlemen." The DJ's voice interrupted her moment, "please welcome for the first time Mr. and Mrs. Devonshire."

The room erupted in clapping and cheers as Gwen and Drew walked over to their table. As soon as they sat down, the waiters began bringing out the dishes. Carrie only picked at the delicious food, afraid if she ate too much that she would bust the seams on her dress. It was already getting uncomfortable just from sitting.

When the bride and groom finished eating, Scott and Carrie each gave their toast, and then Gwen and Drew danced their first dance.

"Come on." Carrie grabbed Philippe's hand when other couples were invited to the floor. This was the moment she had waited for. Carrie loved dancing and Philippe would never indulge her, but surely, he wouldn't say no at a wedding. It was expected guests would dance at a wedding.

"I don't dance," he said with a shake of his head. "I've told you that before."

"I understand, but it's my best friend's wedding. I want to dance at her wedding."

"Two left feet." He pointed to the floor. "Don't like making a fool of myself."

"But what about our-" Carrie snapped her mouth shut. She had been about to ask him about their wedding and he hadn't even proposed yet. She must be caught up in the wedding fever.

"Our what?" he asked.

"Nothing, I'm going to grab some punch." She turned away before the hurt expression on her face displayed her true feelings. If they did marry, would he not dance with her? Surely, he would make an exception for his own wedding.

"May I have this dance?"

Carrie looked to her left to see Max staring at her with his hand outstretched. "No, it's fine, really."

"Come on, Alyssa sent me over here. She's too pregnant to dance. Besides, it might help your man see what he's missing."

Carrie glanced over at Alyssa who smiled and shot her a thumb up sign. "Okay," she said with a laugh. "If it's all right with Alyssa. She's a pretty amazing woman."

Max situated her in his arms when they reached the dance floor. "Don't I know it. She's way too good for me. You know, I never expected I'd marry. I was rather like you - a serial dater, though I wasn't as nice about it. I was pretty awful to the women I dated." He spun her around. "My point is that if I can find love, you can too."

"Thank you." Carrie smiled up at him. He might not have started out a kind man, but he certainly was now.

After Max, she danced with Scott, then Drew, then random guests who came and asked her. It almost seemed as if they were keeping her busy to distract her from remembering her own date's refusal to dance, but Carrie didn't mind. Before she knew it, it was time for the bouquet toss. She lined up with the other women, and Gwen's aim was as true as her word. The bundle of flowers landed squarely in her hands.

"I told you," Gwen said before she was whisked away.

Carrie smiled and then turned to Philippe. She almost laughed at the pained expression on his face as she held up the bouquet. It was a silly tradition, but she couldn't help hoping that maybe catching the bouquet would turn things around for her. With all her friends married or getting married, she was starting to long for that solid foundation as well.

Continue reading The Billionaire's Cowboy Groom…

Or get the boxed set with all 4 books and save 38%

A FREE STORY FOR YOU

*E*njoyed this story? Not ready to quit reading yet? If you sign up for my newsletter, you will receive The Billionaire's Impromptu Bet right away as my thank you gift for choosing to hang out with me.

The Billionaire's Impromptu Bet

A SWAT officer. A bored billionaire heiress. A bet that could change everything….

Read on for a taste of The Billionaire's Impromptu Bet….

*B*rie Carter fell back spread eagle on her queen-sized canopy bed sending her blond hair fanning out behind her. With a large sigh, she uttered, "I'm bored."

"How can you be bored? You have like millions of dollars." Her friend, Ariel, plopped down in a seated position on the bed beside her and flicked her raven hair off her shoulder. "You want to go shopping? I hear Tiffany's is having a special right now."

Brie rolled her eyes. Shopping? Where was the excitement in that? With her three platinum cards, she could go shopping whenever she wanted. "No, I'm bored with shopping too. I have everything. I want to do something exciting. Something we don't normally do."

Brie enjoyed being rich. She loved the unlimited credit cards at her disposal, the constant apparel of new clothes, and of course the penthouse apartment her father paid for, but lately, she longed for something more fulfilling.

Ariel's hazel eyes widened. "I know. There's a new bar down on Franklin Street. Why don't we go play a little game?"

Brie sat up, intrigued at the secrecy and the twinkle in Ariel's eyes. "What kind of game?"

"A betting game. You let me pick out any man in the place. Then you try to get him to propose to you."

Brie wrinkled her nose. "But I don't want to get married." She loved her freedom and didn't want to share her penthouse with anyone, especially some man.

"You don't marry him, silly. You just get him to propose."

Brie bit her lip as she thought. It had been awhile since her last relationship and having a man dote on her for a month might be interesting, but.... "I don't know. It doesn't seem very nice."

"How about I sweeten the pot? If you win, I'll set you up on a date with my brother."

Brie cocked her head. Was she serious? The only thing Brie couldn't seem to buy in the world was the affection of Ariel's very handsome, very wealthy, brother. He was a movie star, just the kind of person Brie could consider marrying in the future. She'd had a crush on him as long as she and Ariel had been friends, but he'd always seen her as just that, his little sister's friend. "I thought you didn't want me dating your brother."

"I don't." Ariel shrugged. "But he's between girlfriends right now, and I know you've wanted it for ages. If you win this bet, I'll set you up. I can't guarantee any more than one date though. The rest will be up to you."

Brie wasn't worried about that. Charm she possessed in abundance. She simply needed some alone time with him, and she was certain she'd be able to convince him they were meant to be together. "All right. You've got a deal."

Ariel smiled. "Perfect. Let's get you changed then and see who the lucky man will be.

A tiny tug pulled on Brie's heart that this still wasn't right, but she dismissed it. This was simply a means to an end, and he'd never have to know.

*J*esse Calhoun relaxed as the rhythmic thudding of the speed bag reached his ears. Though he loved his job, it was stressful being the SWAT sniper. He hated having to take human lives and today had been especially rough. The team had been called out to a drug bust, and Jesse was forced to return fire at three hostiles. He didn't care that they fired at his team and himself first. Taking a life was always hard, and every one of them haunted his dreams.

"You gonna bust that one too?" His co-worker Brendan appeared by his side. Brendan was the opposite of Jesse in nearly every way. Where Jesse's hair was a dark copper, Brendan's was nearly black. Jesse sported paler skin and a dusting of freckles across his nose, but Brendan's skin was naturally dark and freckle free.

Jesse flashed a crooked grin, but kept his eyes on the small, swinging black bag. The speed bag was his way to release, but a few times he had started hitting while still too keyed up and he had ruptured the bag. Okay, five times, but who was counting really? Besides, it was a better way to calm his nerves than other things he could choose. Drinking, fights, gambling, women.

"Nah, I think this one will last a little longer." His shoulders began to burn, and he gave the bag another few punches for good measure before dropping his arms and letting it swing to a stop. "See? It lives to be hit at least another day." Every once in a while, Jesse missed training the way he used to. Before he joined the force, he had been an amateur boxer, on his way to being a pro, but a shoulder injury had delayed his training and forced him to consider something else. It had eventually healed, but by then he had lost his edge.

"Hey, why don't you come drink with us?" Brendan clapped a hand on Jesse's shoulder as they headed into the locker room.

"You know I don't drink." Jesse often felt like the outsider of the team. While half of the six-man team was married, the other half found solace in empty bottles and meaningless relationships. Jesse understood that - their job was such that they never knew if they would come home night after night - but he still couldn't partake.

Brendan opened his locker and pulled out a clean shirt. He peeled off his current one and added deodorant before tugging on the new one. "You don't have to drink. Look, I won't drink either. Just come and hang out with us. You have no one waiting for you at home."

That wasn't entirely true. Jesse had Bugsy, his Boston Terrier, but he understood Brendan's point. Most days, Jesse went home, fed Bugsy, made dinner, and fell asleep watching TV on the couch. It wasn't much of a life. "All right, I'll go, but I'm not drinking."

Brendan's lips pulled back to reveal his perfectly white teeth. He bragged about them, but Jesse knew they were veneers. "That's the spirit. Hurry up and change. We don't want to leave the rest of the team waiting."

"Is everyone coming?" Jesse pulled out his shower necessities. Brendan might feel comfortable going out with just a new application of deodorant, but Jesse needed to wash more than just dirt and sweat off. He needed to wash the sound of the bullets and the sight of lifeless bodies from his mind.

"Yeah, Pat's wife is pregnant again and demanding some crazy food concoctions. Pat agreed to pick them up if she let him have an hour. Cam and Jared's wives are having a girls' night, so the whole gang can be together. It will be nice to hang out when we aren't worried about being shot at."

"Fine. Give me ten minutes. Unlike you, I like to clean up before I go out."

Brendan smirked. "I've never had any complaints. Besides, do you know how long it takes me to get my hair like this?"

Jesse shook his head as he walked into the shower, but he knew it was true. Brendan had rugged good looks and muscles to match. He rarely had a hard time finding a woman. Jesse on the other hand hadn't dated anyone in the last few months. It wasn't that he hadn't been looking, but he was quieter than his teammates. And he wasn't looking for right now. He was looking for forever. He just hadn't found it yet.

Click here to continue reading The Billionaire's Impromptu Bet.

THE STORY DOESN'T END!

You've met a few people and fallen in love....

I bet you're wondering how you can meet everyone else.

Star Lake Series:

When Love Returns: The first in the Star Lake series. Presley Hays and Brandon Scott were best friends in High School until Morgan entered their town and stole Brandon's heart. Devastated, Presley takes a scholarship to Le Cordon Bleu, but five years later, she is back in Star Lake after a tough breakup. Brandon thought he'd never return to Star Lake after Morgan left him and his daughter Joy, but when his father needs help, he returns home and finds more than he bargained for. Can Presley and Brandon forget past hurts or will their stubborn natures keep them apart forever?

Once Upon a Star: The second book in the Star Lake series. Audrey left Star Lake to pursue acting, but after an unplanned pregnancy her jobs and her money dwindled, leaving her no option except to return home and start over. Blake was the quintessential nerd in high school and was never able to tell Audrey how he felt. Now that he's gained confidence and some muscle, will he finally be able to reveal his feelings? Once Upon a Star will take you back to Christmas in Star Lake. Revisit your favorite characters and meet a few ones in this sweet Christmas read.

Love Conquers All: Lanie Perkins Hall never imagined being divorced at thirty. Nor did she imagine falling for an old friend, but when she runs into Azarius Jacobson, she can't deny the attraction. As they begin to spend more time together, Lanie struggles with the fact Azarius keeps his past a secret. What is he hiding? And will she ever be able to get him to open up? Azarius Jacobson has loved Lanie Perkins Hall from the moment he saw her, but issues from his past have left him guarded. Now that he has another chance with her, will he find the courage to share his life with her? Or will his emotional walls create a barrier that will leave him alone once more? Find out in this heartfelt, emotional third book (stand alone) in the Star Lake series.

The Heartbeats Series:

Where It All Began: Sandra Baker thought her life was on the right track until she ended up pregnant. Her boyfriend, not wanting the baby, pushes her to have an abortion. After the procedure, Sandra's life falls apart, and she turns to alcohol. Her relationship ends, and she struggles to find meaning in her life. When she meets Henry Dobbs, a strong Christian man, she begins to wonder if God would accept her. Will she tell Henry her darkest secret? And will she ever be able to forgive herself and find healing? Find out in this emotional love story.

The Power of Prayer: Callie Green thought she had her whole life planned out until her fiance left her at the altar. When her carefully laid plans crumble, she begins to make mistakes at work and engage in uncharacteristic activities. After a mistake nearly costs her her job, she cashes in her honeymoon tickets for some time away. There she meets JD, a charming Christian man who, even though she is not a believer, captures her interest. Before their relationship can deepen, Callie's ex-fiance shows back up in her life and she is forced to choose between Daniel and JD. Who will she choose and how will her choice affect the rest of her life? Find out in this touching novel.

When Hearts Collide: Amanda Adams has always been a Christian, but she's a novice at relationships. When she meets Caleb, her emotions get the best of her and she ignores the sign that something is amiss. Will she find out before it's too late? Jared Masterson is still healing from his girlfriend's strange rejection and disappearance when he meets Amanda. She captivates his heart, but can he save her from making the biggest mistake of her life? A must read for mothers and daughters. Though part of the series and the first of the college spin off series, it is a stand alone book and can be read separately.

A Past Forgiven: Jess Peterson has lived a life of abuse and lost her self worth, but when she is paired with a Christian roommate, she begins to wonder if there is a loving father looking down on her. Her decisions lead her one way, but when she ends up pregnant, she must make some major changes. Chad Michelson is healing from his own past and uses meaningless relationships to hide his pain, but when Jess becomes pregnant, he begins to wonder about the meaning of life. Can he step up and be there for Jess and the baby?

Sweet Billionaires Series:

The Billionaire's Secret: Maxwell Banks was the ultimate player until he found himself caring for a daughter he didn't know he had. Can he change to become the role model she needs? Alyssa Miller hasn't had the best luck with past relationships, so why is she falling for the one man who is sure to break her heart? Though nearly complete opposites, feelings develop, but can Max really change his philandering ways? Or will one mistake seal his fate forever?

A Brush with a Billionaire: Brent just wanted to finish his novel in peace, but when his car breaks down in Sweet Grove, he is forced to deal with a female mechanic and try to get along. Sam thought she had given up on city boys, but when Brent shows up in her shop, she finds herself fighting attraction. Will their stubborn natures keep them apart or can a small town festival bring them together?

The Billionaire's Christmas Miracle: Drew Devonshire is captivated by the woman he meets at a masquerade ball, but who is she? Gwen Rodgers is a teacher, but when she pretends to be her friend and meets Drew at a masquerade ball, her world gets thrown upside down.

The Billionaire's Cowboy Groom: Carrie Bliss finally found the man she wants to marry but there's just one little problem. She's technically still married. Cal Roper hasn't seen her in years but his heart still belongs to his wife. When she returns to town requesting a divorce, can he convince her they belong together?

The Cowboy Billionaire: Coming Soon!

The Lawkeeper Series:

Lawfully Matched: Kate Whidby doesn't want to impose on her newly married brother after their parents die, so she accepts a mail order bride offer in the paper. Little does she know the man she intends to marry has a dark past, sending her fleeing into a neighboring town and into Jesse Jenning's life. Jesse never wanted to be in law enforcement, but after a band of robbers kills his fiancee, he dons the badge and swears revenge. Will he find his fiancee's killer? And when Kate flies into his life, will he be able to put his painful past behind him in order to love again?

Lawfully Justified: William Cook turns to bounty hunting after losing his wife. When he suffers a life-threatening injury, he is forced to stay in town with an intriguing woman. Emma Stewart has moved back in with her widowed father, the town doctor, but she still longs for a family of her own, so no one is more surprised than she is when she starts to develop feeling for the bounty hunter, who hides his heart of gold behind a rugged exterior. Can Emma offer William a reason to stay? Can William find a way to heal from his broken past to start a future with Emma? Or will a haunting secret take away all the possibilities of this budding romance?

The Scarlet Wedding: William and Emma are planning their wedding, but an outbreak and a return from his past force them to change their plans. Is a happily ever after still in their future?

Lawfully Redeemed: Dani Higgins is a K9 cop looking to make a name for herself, but she finds herself at the mercy of a stranger after an accident. Calvin Phillips just wanted to help his brother, but somehow he ended up in the middle of a police investigation and caring for the woman trying to bring his brother in.

The Still Small Voice Series:

The Still Small Voice: Jordan Wright was searching for something after she gave her son up for adoption. What she found was God, and she began receiving visions. But can she trust Him when he asks her to do something big? Kat Jameson had long been a lukewarm Christian, but when her friend dies and she begins seeing lights, she thinks she is going crazy. Then she meets someone with a message for her. Will she be able to give up control and do what is asked of her?

A Spark in the Darkness coming soon!

Blushing Brides Series:

The Cowboy's Reality Bride: Tyler Hall just wanted to find love, but the women he dated wanted more than his small-town life provided. He gets more than he bargained for when he ends up on a reality dating show and falls for a woman who is not a contestant. Laney Swann has been running from her past for years, but it takes meeting a man on a reality dating show to make her see there's no need to run.

The Reality Bride's Baby: Laney wants nothing more than a baby, but when she starts feeling dizzy is it pregnancy or something more serious?

The Producer's Unlikely Bride: Justin Miller had given up on love, but when his image needs help, he finds himself needing the aid of a stranger who just happens to be a romance writer. Ava McDermott is waiting for the perfect love, but after agreeing to a fake relationship with Justin, she finds herself falling for real.

Ava's Blessing in Disguise: Five years after marriage, Ava faces a mysterious illness that threatens to ruin her career. Will she find out what it is?

The Soldier's Steadfast Bride: coming soon

The Men of Fire Beach

Fire Games: Cassidy returns home from Who Wants to Marry a Cowboy to find obsessive letters from a fan. The cop assigned to help her wants to get back to his case, but what she sees at a fire may just be the key he's looking for.

Lost Memories and New Beginnings: coming soon

Stand Alones:

Love Renewed: This books is part of the multi author second chance series. When fate reunites high school sweethearts separated by life's choices, can they find a second chance at love at a snowy lodge amid a little mystery?

Her children's early reader chapter book series:
    The Wishing Stone #1: Dangerous Dinosaur
    The Wishing Stone #2: Dragon Dilemma
    The Wishing Stone #3: Mesmerizing Mermaids
    The Wishing Stone #4: Pyramid Puzzle
    The Wishing Stone Inspirations 1: Mary's Miracle
    To see a list of all her books

authorloranahoopes.com
loranahoopes@gmail.com

ABOUT THE AUTHOR

Lorana Hoopes is an inspirational author originally from Texas but now living in the PNW with her husband and three children. When not writing, she can be seen kickboxing at the gym, singing, or acting on stage. One day, she hopes to retire from teaching and write full time.